X X X

I moan into Ty's mouth as he finally kicks up our session a notch and frees my breast from the confines of my bra, massaging it in circles, digging the metal of his rings into the soft flesh. I sigh against him, relaxing my body and dropping my hands, sensing Ty's need to be in control. I have no problem surrendering to him. That's what love is really. Surrendering yourself to the person that means the most to you. Appropriate or not, a piece of Noah's poetry sounds in my head, the perfect lyrics to the song Ty and I are singing with our bodies. It's another line from *For Them The Wheel Turned,* the very same poem I was quoting to myself when Ty first took me to SOG. Talk about coming full circle.

And the unwashed found refuge in capitulation; and they were ecstatic in their state because it made them bigger than the self; connecting them to their other halves, this process built hearts and souls and became their reason for living.

X X X

Books by C.M. Stunich

The Seven Wicked Series
First
Second
Third
Fourth
Fifth
Sixth
Seventh

Houses Novels
The House of Gray and Graves
The House of Hands and Hearts and Hair
The House of Sticks and Bones

Indigo Lewis Novels
Indigo & Iris
Indigo & The Colonel
Indigo & Lynx

The Huntswomen Trilogy
The Feed
The Hunt
The Throne

Never say Never Trilogy
Tasting Never
Finding Never
Keeping Never

She Lies Twisted

Hell Inc.

DeadBorn

A Werewolf Christmas (A Short Story)

Broken Pasts

Fuck Valentine's Day

Clan of the Griffin Riders: Chryer's Crest

Keeping Never

C.M. STUNICH

SARIAN ROYAL

Keeping Never
Copyright © C.M. Stunich

"Paint Me Beautiful" Excerpt Copyright © C.M. Stunich

All rights reserved. Printed in the United States of America. No part of this book may be used or reproduced in any manner whatsoever without written permission except in the case of brief quotations embodied in critical articles or reviews. For information address Sarian Royal Indie Publishing, 1863 Pioneer Pkwy. E Ste. 203, Springfield, OR 97477-3907.
www.sarianroyal.com

ISBN-10: 1938623495 (pbk.)
ISBN-13: 978-1-938623-49-3 (pbk.)

Edited By Brandy Little of "Little Bee's Editing Services"
Cover art and design © Amanda Carroll and Sarian Royal
Optimus Princeps font © Manfred Klein
Conrad Veidt © Bumbayo Font Fabrik

The characters and events portrayed in this book are fictitious. Any similarity to real persons, living or dead, businesses, or locales is coincidental and is not intended by the author.

*to the ones who Never lose hope,
no matter how hard things get.
Lauren Dootson, that means you!*

1

I'm keeping a secret from my soul mate.

It's not an easy decision to live with and it's reduced my nails to mere stubs and turned my fingers raw and bloody as I chew at them nervously. All the while, my sea blue ring, the one that sparkles with Ty's heart and the best laid plans of men, shines bright in my vision and makes my eyes water even now.

Seriously, Never, don't be such a fucking coward. I sigh and drop my hands to my lap, determined to get some hot sauce or something, anything to keep them out of my mouth. The thought of spicy food makes my stomach turn, and I barely make it to the bathroom before I'm puking my guts out and silently cursing Ty. *You should've known,* I tell myself as I sit back against the bathroom cabinet and try to breathe through my nose. *Guys like that always succeed the first time. Fucking stud.*

"Hey." I jump and my eyes snap open, slide up Ty's long legs and get caught on his new lip ring. It's gold with a green gem in the center, and sort of reminds me of St. Patrick's Day. Still, he looks hot in it. Ty always looks hot. "Beth wants to know if we're opening any presents tomorrow evening?"

"Huh?" I ask as I put the butt of my hand to my head and wish like crazy for a cigarette. I never realized it before, but smoking was like a breathing exercise for me. *In. Out. In. Out.* It was one of the things that kept me from hyperventilating which is what I feel like doing now. I want to open up my mouth and blurt my secret out right now, let it float in the air like a butterfly and land on Ty's lips where it will rest in suspended silence until the end of time.

Ty senses something is wrong – he always does – and leans against the door frame, popping a cigarette in his mouth. My eyes follow the tip of it as he talks and it jiggles around enticingly. I feel like a dog at the racetrack, like I would run all damn day for a single drag.

"Let's talk about it," he says, and I know that he's just speculating.

"Talk about what?" I say as I examine my ring and smile. Yesterday, Ty asked me to marry him, and I said yes. We haven't told anyone about it yet, but we're going to tomorrow, on Christmas Eve. It's all so fairy tale that it kind of makes me want to roll my eyes, but at the same time, it's so sweet that I can't possibly act like I'm not affected by the gesture.

"Well ... " Ty drawls as he glances over his shoulder for signs of my sisters. When he doesn't find anyone, he lights up and closes his eyes in bliss, taking a drag and pulling the cig from his mouth with two fingers. I practically drool and have to turn my head to stare at the bit of mold that's starting to creep up from beneath the baseboards. Not good. "You keep throwing up, so something must be wrong."

"I'm on my period," I say because that makes so much fucking sense. When I glance back at Ty, I see that his dark brows are raised skeptically.

"Uh huh," he says as he puts the cigarette back to his lips, bracelets jingling like summer wind chimes. "Because a woman's menstrual cycle frequently comes without blood and with a whole shit ton of puking."

"Thanks for making me feel so attractive," I say as I stand up and turn around to face the sink. Ty steps inside behind me and closes the door with his foot, sliding his arms over my shoulders and down my chest. He rests his chin against my shoulder and lets the smoke from his cig trail out and tickle my nose. I take a big, guilty inhale and try not to think about all the horrible things it may or may not do to this baby that I may or may not keep.

The longer you wait to talk to Ty, the harder this will be, dumb ass.

"I find you very attractive," he says and drops the cigarette purposely into the still running water of the sink, stepping back and grabbing my hips with his hands. "Want me to show you exactly how much?" He pauses and then adds, "The future Mrs. McCabe."

"Right," I say as I resist the urge to give into him and let myself go. Ty makes me feel like that, and I think that's one of the reasons I like him so much. He makes me want to split my body open and release my soul, let it fly and not care how black it is, how tarnished. Despite what I might say, Ty really does make me feel beautiful, inside and out. "Who says I'm changing my name?"

"Aw," Ty says as he spins me around and kisses me quick and sharp on the lips. "But I want to have the same last name as you."

"Change yours," I say with a shrug, but I don't think 'Ty Ross' has the same ring as 'Ty McCabe'.

"Never!" There's a banging at the door. It's Lettie. "Beth says that if she catches you smoking, she's going to ring your neck."

I sigh and put one hand on my hip, just so Ty knows he's in trouble.

"Sorry, baby," he tells me and presses the sweetest, softest kiss to my mouth, hot and perfect. How can I stay mad? *How can I continue to lie?*

"I love you, Ty McCabe," I say as he smiles and draws some hair behind my ear with his fingers.

"I love you, too, Never Ross."

2

Noah Scott comes over for Christmas Eve which is fine because nobody knows what happened between us in the kitchen that day, the way he said goodbye, the way he gave me up for good.

"Hi Never," he says as he scoots in the front door and shakes snow from his boots. "Merry Christmas, Ty."

"Merry X to the Mass," Ty says which is weird but kind of cute. Noah notices my ring right away though I'm not wearing it on my ring finger; it's on my middle. He stares at it for a long time and then slides his blue, blue eyes up to Ty's dark ones, pauses there and smiles. It's a sad smile, but a real one.

"I brought some gifts over, but I left them in the car. Do you think you could help me carry them in?" I open my mouth to reply, but Ty beats me to it, stepping forward and bending down to grab his combat boots.

"Yup," is all he says as he stands up and kisses my cheek gently, lip ring brushing against my flesh, warm and hard. "Be right back, babe." I sigh, but I don't say anything. What is there to say, really? My first love and my true love are spending a holiday together with me and my recently repaired family. Ty and Noah escape outside without getting caught by any of the little ones. All they want to do is play in the snow, but Beth, in all of her motherliness, has said it's too harsh out right now, and I can't disagree. Snow is falling in crooked sheets, blanketing the ground with soft pillows of white that have already toppled some of the weaker trees in the area and snapped off limbs from the strongest. *We'll go outside eventually,* she tells them, *eventually but not now.*

"Hey." I turn around and see Zella standing next to the staircase with Beth. She's grinding her lip between her teeth nervously. I step forward and push the door closed to keep the chill winter wind out. In her eyes, I see my secret burning hot and fierce. She is *this* close to blurting it out for the world to hear.

"Zella, no," I say, but she moves forward and hugs me, pulls me against her warm chest, squeezes me like we're as close now as we were when I left, maybe closer. It's a nice feeling, but a hard one to understand. How can she forgive me so easily when I'm barely figuring out how to forgive myself?

"I'm so happy for you, Never," she says. "You and Ty will make cute, little babies." I sigh and push back from her, certain that I don't want to have this conversation right here, right now. My life is structured so that were I to say something back, Ty would walk in at that exact moment and find out in the worst way possible. In fact, *finding out* is not an option. If he *finds out,* and I don't actually *tell* him, then I'm in big time trouble. Ty McCabe will be fucking pissed off. There is no doubt in my mind about that.

"That's enough, Zella," I say and my tone, while not harsh, is no-nonsense, kind of like Beth's. *Hell, I'm getting started on my mother voice already. Nice.* "Ty doesn't know." Zella nods and tosses a casual glance over her shoulder at Beth who looks guilty enough that I don't get mad at her.

"I had to tell someone," Beth says, and her facial expression is so tense and distracted that you'd think she was the one who was pregnant. I watch her carefully for a moment. "I was digging out baby clothes from the closet and … " I nod and wave my hand. I don't need her to explain herself. My family's had enough of that. We need to keep up with this forward momentum of understanding and forgiveness. After all, that's what life is all about. Martin Luther King, Jr. said it best. *Darkness cannot drive out darkness; only light can do that. Hate cannot drive out hate; only love can do that.*

"It's fine," I say and then, as I hear footsteps on the deck, I add, "As long as you keep it to yourself."

"Ho ho ho," Ty says as he kicks open the door and steps inside with an armful of colorful gifts. Noah has taken the time to wrap each one in a different patterned paper, and there are bows and ribbons and glitter galore. "It's Santa fucking Claus!"

"Language," Beth says quickly, although she won't scold Ty if he does it again. She never scolds Ty. "What is all this?"

"I'm sorry," Noah says as he follows in behind Ty and sets

down some pink and yellow boxes next to the door. "I got a bit carried away."

"Presents!" Lorri shouts as she skids across the wood floor in slipper socks and throws her arms around Noah's legs. "Yay!" Noah laughs and ruffles her hair, and I can't help but think how much easier this would all be if I was in love with Noah. Noah has money, family, connections. Ty has ... a hot, fucking body, eyes that burn, and a soul that's blacker than coal but just as warm. I sigh.

"Go for a smoke with me?" he asks as he passes by and goes into the living room, depositing his load of presents next to the tree. I don't answer him, but I do catch the eyes of both Beth and Zella on my way out. Two pairs of hazel orbs tell me without words, *Don't you dare.* I know without a doubt that there is no way I'm letting my shit fuck up my baby before it's even born. *If it's born.* I shiver and grab my coat, follow Ty out the door and watch as he digs out a box of cigs. He stares at it for a moment and then pulls back his arm and chucks the red and white rectangle out into the snow. Ty's bracelets jingle like bells as he drops his hand back to his side.

"What the hell?" I ask as I gape at him and he shrugs nonchalantly.

"Want to quit with me?" he asks and as I stare at him, a wave of nausea takes over me and I suddenly just feel so freaking *tired,* like I could just curl up on the porch swing and fall asleep watching the snow. I put out a hand and touch the side of the house for support. Black and red hair falls over my face, reminding me that I need to make a decision about those copper roots. It's metaphorical somehow, spiritual in a way. It might just be hair, but it means something.

"Are you shitting me?" I ask, wondering what might happen if we both quit at the same time. Two chain smokers going cold turkey. We'll be at each other's throats. "No!" Ty sweeps the curtain of my hair away with his ringed fingers.

"Come on, Nev," he says as his dark eyes bore into my soul and make me dizzy. Or maybe that's just his baby growing inside me, the one he doesn't know about. "We're making all kinds of new starts here, why not add one more?"

"Go pick up the box," I say to him as I do my best to hold back a wave of puke. It's this bad and I'm barely pregnant. Does it get worse? My stomach roils and I close my eyes. *How much worse could it possibly get?* Ty chuckles and his laugh weaves into the cracks of my psyche and warms me up from the inside out.

"I was going to pick it up, yeah. I respect the earth, baby. I just threw it for dramatic effect."

"Go to hell," I tell him, and he kisses me on the lips, nice and soft, like he's trying to mimic the gentle drift of the falling snow. "I bet you a hundred bucks you can't go more than a week without smoking."

"You don't have a hundred bucks," Ty says and I stand up straight, and narrow my eyes at him. "But I'll bet you a nasty, dirty, pervy favor that I can. And hey, if you look at it right, no matter what happens, we both win."

"You're on," I say and watch as he trudges through the snow and retrieves the box of cigarettes, tucking them in his back pocket at the same moment his phone rings. It hardly ever goes off; after all, Ty is like me in every which way and he has as many friends as I do. That is to say, none. Well, before me. I'd like to consider myself his friend. And maybe Lacey. She's the only person I've told about my engagement. I was so excited after it happened that when we came back from the cemetery, I locked myself in my bathroom and called her. She was as thrilled about that as she was about the baby. Seems like everyone that knows is excited. Everyone but me. What am I going to do with a baby?

Tell him now, before he finds out and you scar him beyond saving, Never Ross.

I look at Ty whose dark hair looks so soft and perfect, coated with tiny, white flakes of sky that melt as quickly as they come and drip down his nose and catch on his lip ring. When he comes back up this porch, I can spit out my secret with two little words. *I'm pregnant.* I square my shoulders and take a deep breath. I've survived hell. I've traveled to the depths of my own soul, found the darkness crouching there, and faced it head on. Not many can say they've done that. Now, all I need to do is tell the father of my baby that I'm carrying a piece of him inside of me, and see what he thinks we should do. I tell myself that I haven't told him because he's going to freak, because he can't handle it, but what I really think is that *I* can't handle it. I'm the one with the issues, not him. In my heart, I know that when I tell Ty, he's going to smile, take my face in his strong hands and kiss me. Whether he'll be a good father or not, I don't know because I don't really know what a good father is, but he's a perfect soul mate. That should be enough for me. *I can do this,* I think as I watch him crunch back towards me. It takes me a minute to figure out that there's something wrong, but when I see the blank look in my future husband's eyes, I know the worst that could possibly happen just has. That the one thing that could punish us both, erase the blackboard of our new lives, has just crept up and bit him.

Ty's past is back.

"What's wrong?" I ask as I step forward and grab his arm. It takes Ty several seconds to look over at me, to tug at his already bleeding lip ring with his teeth. I reach up and cover it with two fingers, try to still his nervous habit.

"I got a phone call," he begins, and I don't rush him. "It was from my mother."

3

Ty stands like a zombie on that porch. His eyes are dead and his muscles are tense. He's squeezing his hands into tight fists that make his knuckles as white as the snow at our feet.

"Your mother?" I ask, wondering how she got his number. Ty's already told me that he has no contact with the woman who birthed him, who raised him. *What if my kid leaves me like that? What if I hurt her or him the same way Ty was hurt?* I have to blink several times to keep the creeping demons of doubt back. Obviously, I can't spill my secret now. It's not an excuse, just a fact. I mean, if I were to tell Ty now, would he even hear me? His eyes are glassy and empty, and it's a hard sight to see.

"Sorry, not her exactly, just her ghost." *Shit,* I think. *Ty McCabe has fucking lost it. It's just a matter of time before I go, too.* I drop my hand from his face and turn to look at the front door as it opens and a copper haired head pokes out.

"Beth wants to talk to you, Never," Lettie says as her eyes swing over to Ty's face and freeze there. I see right away that she senses a change in him. It's like some switch has been flicked in Ty's brain. It's turned off that fire, that light, that energy and left him blank. I have to shake him out of it and quick. I once saw this girl use a little, plastic clicker on a frightened dog. It was pulling on its leash, flailing around like a mad thing. She clicked the device and its ears snapped forward; its eyes swung over to her face. I decide that Ty is much the same as that dog in this moment. He isn't thinking clearly, and it's my job to snap him out of it. A slap is out of the question, so I maneuver myself in front of him and clap my hands hard and sharp. Works like a charm. After all, inside of each of us is a frightened animal waiting to take over and send us over the edge.

Ty blinks at me carefully and then folds his hands over his mouth in a steepled position.

"Ty … " I begin and then glance over my shoulder at Lettie who's still staring at Ty with a curious expression on her young face. She doesn't understand the pain she sees in him, and I hope she never does. "Tell Beth I'll be there in a minute," I say and when Lettie doesn't retreat, I raise my eyebrows and purse my lips. Little kids are excellent at reading body language. It's a skill that slowly disappears as we get older, but one that I think the world would benefit from nurturing.

So much can be said with a raised brow or a tense jaw, a tilted head, a firm set to one's shoulders. Lettie sighs and retreats, letting the screen door slam behind her. She doesn't bother to close the front door which makes me nervous. My family is notoriously nosy, and I know somehow, just *know*, that Noah Scott is listening, too. I turn back to my bad boy, my heart throb, panty dropping, butterfly whose smile makes me weak in the knees and whose eyes burn me from the inside out and cleanse my pain each and every time I look at him. I turn back to him and I ask, "What's going on?" See, I know nothing about Ty's past, nothing at all. He's got all the gory, dirty details of my life spelled out in blood and I have nothing on him but the whispers of ghosts. He doesn't like his mom; she took pictures of cars; he stole her rings. Other than that, I've got nothing.

"My mother's in the hospital," Ty says, and then he drops his hands and turns around, sitting down on the porch swing heavy and hard like his legs have just given out, crippled by the weight of this revelation. "That was actually her *lawyer* on the phone. He says she's pretty much dead and that if I want to see her before she goes that I better get my butt up to New York." I don't know what to say (which seems to happen a lot lately), so I just sit down next to Ty and take his butterflies in my hand, brush my fingers over his skin. It's all smooth up his arm and though I've never seen him do it, I think he shaves, so that the tattoos are as bright and crisp as can be. What do you say to someone who hates their last, dying family member?

"Would you like to go see her?" I ask. Ty laughs, harsh and hard, like I haven't heard in awhile. If I'm being honest with myself, I have to say that it's a little scary.

"Fuck no," he says and then pulls his hand from mine so he can drop his face into his palms with a groan. "Honestly, I hope that cancer has rotted her from the inside out."

"Ty," I begin because I know how hard it is to hold onto that hate. Even now, on this Christmas Eve, this momentous moment when all her family is gathered in one, single spot for the first time in years, the first time in Maple and Darla's existence, my mother is heading out the front door and giving me and Ty a cursory glance that's as empty as Ty's were when he got his phone call. My mother (I use this term loosely) has on a pair of bright, red boots with heels that are inappropriate for the snowy weather and a short, black dress that peeks out from beneath her winter coat. Her makeup is too thick and she looks like one of the dime a dozen whores that work the streets across the road from Ty's apartment. Today, she's heading over to her boyfriend's house. He has a child of his own and wants to spend the day with her and his parents. My mother chooses this over us, chooses to go to them instead of bringing them to us. We hardly factor into her decisions.

"Merry Christmas," I say randomly. This stops her on the bottom step for a moment.

"Don't forget to unplug the lights on the tree before you go to bed. The house isn't insured. If we lose it, those of us who aren't running back to California after the holidays are going to be homeless." And then she starts moving towards her old, beat up station wagon, the same one that she used to cart us around in as kids. Like I said, there's not much money in the belly dancing industry, especially not for a washed up, evil, old bitch like Angelica.

"Hey," Ty says and my mother ignores him, slipping and sliding across the icy snow in her stupid boots. "Fuck you." I laugh, can't help it, and I find myself looking over at Ty who's nibbling his lip hard and glaring at my mom with steely eyes that show her no sympathy, that refuse to cloak her selfish insecurities and foolish decisions in anything but shame. "You have a daughter that was willing to give you another chance.

Do you know how lucky you are?"

"I want you out of my house by the time I get back," Angelica tells Ty as she slips and lands on her ass in the slushy, muddy mess that surrounds her car. Neither of us move to help her up.

"If Ty goes, I go," I say, and it's as simple as that. I take his hand in mine and give it a squeeze. True to my words, Beth proves that she has, indeed, been listening in on Ty and my conversation and comes out onto the porch, crossing her arms over her chest rather authoritatively.

"I pay all the taxes. I pay the electricity. I pay the water. *And,* despite your belief to the contrary, I also pay the home insurance. Your name might be on the papers, but this house is mine. They stay."

"Oh for Christ's sake, Beth," Angelica says as she uses the handle of the car door to stand herself up. "You're as dramatic as your sister." And then she gets in and drives away. Beth says nothing, but she does pause on her way back inside to squeeze my shoulder.

"It's cold out here. You almost ready to come inside? I actually have an announcement I want to make." My eyes snap up to hers and pause there, trying to read her emotions. She's not going to talk about my pregnancy is she? No, that isn't it. Whatever it is that Beth has to say, it's about her own life, not mine. I study her carefully and nod, glad that I have a big sister with a heart that's all encompassing, that looks at me with as much love as she looks at her own daughter. I am so, so lucky.

"Fifteen minutes," I say and she nods, tucking some of her short, copper hair behind one ear. She understands, I know she does. When Beth goes back in, she closes the front door behind her to give Ty and me some privacy.

"Want and need," Ty begins as his gaze travels up to the

sky and focuses on the slices of snow that cut through the gray and twirl like ballerinas, melding into the flow of frozen water like the most perfectly choreographed troupe. *Beautiful.* "Two totally different fucking things. Don't you hate how they're always at each other's throats?" I don't answer him, quite aware that whatever it is that he's talking about, it's more for his benefit than it is for mine. One thing I do know: if Ty goes to New York, I go to New York. Period. "I don't want to see my mother, but I think I need to, right?" Again, I remain silent. He needs to figure this out for himself. I did, and it nearly broke me, but with Ty's help, I'm healing. It's his turn to break and my turn to repair him. I have to do right by him.

This boy, this Mr. McCabe, is my redemption. I cannot fuck this up.

"I love you," I say simply. "And I know you'll make the right decision, no matter how hard it is, no matter if it cuts you into pieces, because you have to believe that I'll be there for you in the end." Ty squeezes my hand, pulls it to his lips and kisses it with a butterfly's soft touch.

"Wear a white dress for me?" Ty asks, and although his gaze is still dark and his eyes are swimming with fear, he seems a bit more like himself.

"White is for virgins," I say. "And liars. I'm neither of those things." As soon as I say it, as soon as Ty laughs and smiles a sad, dimple free smile, I feel sick. If I do not tell him about this baby, then I am a fucking liar, through and through. I'm breaking the one, golden rule that Ty and I have set for one another. I lick my lips and try to search my lover's facial expression for proof that this is a good time, that this is okay now, but I don't want his thoughts and feelings and decisions tainted by pain and confusion and hurt, uncertainty and old demons. "Okay," I say with a sigh. "White. Off-white, but you're wearing a tux."

Ty's dimples flicker for a moment and disappear into the lush, perfection that is his face. At least his mother gave him that. Ty is a beautiful specimen of humanity. He taps the box of rescued cigarettes against his palm a couple of times and says, "Can I quit tomorrow?" I smile at him and nod, watching as he slides out my favorite forbidden treat and places it between his lips. When Ty goes to light up, his hands shake, and I'm forced to take the lighter from him and flick the silver wheel. Flame sprouts from my fingers as I lift the purple plastic to my lover's mouth and watch the tip of his cig catch. I take a cigarette, too, and put it between my lips, letting it hang there like somehow it will help my cravings.

"If I don't see her, I'll always hate her like this, won't I?" I nod, but that's all I do. Ty is working his way through this, piece by piece. "Fuck me, Never, this sucks."

"Life sucks," I say as Ty pulls out his cig and looks over at me, bracelets tinkling.

"Not when I'm with you," he says, and that's God's honest truth.

4

Ty tells me he still wants to announce our engagement, but I can see that his mind is preoccupied with his mother and how exactly he's going to get to her from here. He says he has to leave in the morning after presents which sucks but which I totally understand. After all, if we go all the way there and find that the source of his hurt and his pain has already left this earth, I don't know what he'll do.

"I hate ham," Lorri says when Beth presents her prize dish

on a silver platter, and I do a big sister thing that I haven't been able to do in years and kick her under the table.

"It looks beautiful, Beth," says Zella who is sitting way too close to Noah Scott, so close that their elbows bump together when they reach out for their water glasses. He is left handed and she's right. It's kind of cute and although I'm still unreasonably attached to Mr. Scott, I can see that Zella is dying for him to notice her in a different way. *Pen pal* is not the title my sister wants to hold in the mind of the blonde haired, blue eyed boy who told me goodbye, but whose eyes can't stop fixating on my sea blue ring, the one that sits pretty next to the other that Ty gave me the night I went to dinner with my sisters. If he keeps presenting me with such prizes, eventually we'll look like twins, both ringed, both damaged, both repaired. And I haven't told him yet, but I want some tattoos. *Guess that's out the window right now. Prego bitches can't get inked.* I shift uncomfortably.

"Before we eat," Beth begins, wringing her hands and looking positively *trashed*. "I have an announcement I want to make." My big sister looks over at me with her pretty, Barbie face, the one that looks so much better when she cries, the one that reminds me somehow of the dad I barely knew and says, *Sorry Never* with a few, well placed blinks. I can't figure out what's going on, so I stay quiet and wait. She doesn't know that Ty and I are together, so she can't possibly know that I was seconds away from making a statement of my own to the family. Maple babbles nonsensically and Darla says *turkey, turkey, turkey* over and over. Still, the atmosphere is pleasant enough. Maybe she got a new job? A new boyfriend? A scholarship?

"I'm pregnant again," she blurts, quite unceremoniously, and the room goes quiet. "With Maple's father." *Ah,* I think as I stare at her with my emotions running wild, *the prick who barely said hi to my sister, who seemed pissed off that he had to take his baby daughter for a night.* I thank my mom for poisoning our blood with a bad taste for men and count my lucky stars that I found Ty. He's one in a million, a shot in the dark, a tortured soul with redeemable qualities and a heart that's too big for this world of hate and pain and angst. "And he's asked me to marry him. He's coming over soon."

"What?!" This from Jade. She stands up and her chair goes toppling over, smashing into the wall and making both Maple and Darla cry. "You didn't say yes to that fuckwad, did you?" she screeches and for once, I think her outburst is well deserved. Here Beth looks guilty and ashamed which freaks me the fuck out because that's how our mother always looked when she was introducing us to new boyfriends that we knew weren't going to stay or who were obviously bad news. Shit.

"I said maybe," Beth says as she picks up her daughter in one arm and pats her little sister's head with her other hand.

"Beth," India begins and her voice is so soft and pretty, such a counterpoint to Jade's yelling that it makes my ears hurt. "You have to say no to him." India looks up at Beth and I watch as something passes between them, something that I don't know. I feel a twinge of jealously and have to calmly remind myself that Rome wasn't built in a day. I can't have perfect, secret free relationships with my sisters when I've only just returned. Life doesn't work like that. When Beth was dating Maple's father, I wasn't around, so I don't know what transpired, but if India is willing to give Beth an order like that, then it must have been seriously harsh.

My stomach roils and I have to put a hand to my mouth to keep from throwing up. From Beth's photo album, I know that she's one of those perfect women who glow when they're pregnant and never get tired, who take up herb gardening and learn to speak a second language during their nine months of incubation. Unfortunately, something in our gene pool must've gotten real screwed up because I'm only a few weeks along and already, I'm sick as a damn dog and *tired* as hell. The way my luck runs, I'll probably be on bed rest for the last few months of this journey. *If you keep it, that is.* I swallow hard. That icky, little thought keeps plaguing my mind, and I can't confront it until I talk to Ty, so I push it back.

"I don't know how," Beth admits openly, and the display of raw emotion on my sister's face causes both Ty and Noah to turn away and look at the floor, like maybe they shouldn't be a part of this. I feel a niggling urge to join them, but I force my eyes to remain on Beth's, watching as any hope of a joyous engagement between Ty and I goes out the window. There is no way in hell I can tell them now. *Circumstance and happenstance, fuck you.*

"You tell that abusive bastard to back off and to shove this stupid ham up his own ass!" Jade yells and then she's turning and marching out the archway to the hallway. Her steps sound loud and heavy as she retreats up the stairs and takes refuge in her bedroom of band posters and cannabis incense. *There goes our happy Christmas,* I think as Beth sits down heavy and sad in her chair and starts to apologize profusely for doing nothing wrong.

"I shouldn't have told you all this way," she begins and India interrupts her gently.

"Beth, it's your life, so you get to decide what happens in it. The mistakes are yours to make." And then she, too, gets up in retreat.

The ham sits forlornly in the center of the table and Beth begins to cry. Zella and I exchange a look across the table and we both know it's up to us to rescue the remainder of this dinner. After all, the little ones have done nothing wrong and poor Ty and poor Noah.

"Shall I cut the roast beast?" I joke as I poke Lorri in the arm. Her face lights up instantly, making me believe all of that crap about children and innocence and whatnot. Fortunately, with my forced joyousness and Zella's terrible jokes, we manage to survive the rest of our meal without anymore heartbreak. India and Jade never rejoin us, and we make a unanimous decision not to open any presents without them.

Still, all is not well in the Ross-Regali household because I still haven't told anyone about Ty's mom, about how after so long apart, I'm leaving on the first real Christmas these girls have had in years. There's that and then there's *this*. I touch my still flat belly and gaze at my eyes in the mirror. They seem brighter somehow, like the flecks of green are shining, giving me the look of someone who has hope. I lift my engagement ring up to my mouth and kiss it gently, imagining that the warm metal is actually Ty, that I'm giving him my soul in my breath, breathing my secrets into his body, lifting this burden from my shoulders.

"Asshat Danny is here," Ty says, barging in without even the courtesy of a knock. Luckily, I'm not doing anything suspect. I glare at him anyway. "And Nev, you know how some people have a gay-dar?" he asks and my eyebrows go up to tickle my hairline. Ty pulls a cigarette out of his pocket and teases me with the tip, talking around the little, white stick and letting it jiggle enticingly. If he keeps doing that, I'm not going to last a week let alone eight more months. Sigh.

"You think Danny is gay?" I ask and Ty shakes his head, ruffling his dark hair with one hand and casting a quick glance down the hall. He looks extra sweaty and tense right now, and his pupils are bigger than normal, dilated with a bit of fear and a dash of anxiety.

"Um, not exactly. I don't really have a gay-dar, but I have

a fucktard-dar, and this guy definitely fits the bill. He is bad news, like headliner bad. If I were you, I'd get Beth out before she climbs so far into her own ass that she can't see the looks on her children's faces when ... " Ty trails off suddenly and although he *sounds* like the man I fell in love with, says things that that man would say, he isn't that man, not right now. Right now he is an abused and abandoned boy, one whose mother chose not to believe him. It's hard to understand how much trust matters. Until someone you count on denies you that, it's impossible to understand where Ty and I come from, how we've grown, where the seeds of our pain were planted. "I'm rambling," he says suddenly, snapping us both back to reality. "Anyway, I don't like what I see playing out in that foyer. She's afraid of him, Never."

"Okay," I say simply because I have to see the situation for myself before I judge. I hated Danny when I met him briefly before. If he's going to be staying for an extended period of time, hate might become *loathe,* and when I loathe, I get angry. *Let it go, Never,* I say to myself. *Just let it go.*

"Danny," Beth says, trying to smile when she sees me coming down the hallway with Ty McCabe at my back, hands tucked into his pockets, head tilted to the side. "This is Never. I believe you met her before?" *Yeah,* I think as I reach out a hand and study the one that grasps it with dry, smooth fingers. *I did, but you never introduced us, and he didn't inquire about me. Hell, he didn't even say hello to you.*

"Nice to meet you, Never," Danny says, ignoring my sister's question in a subtle show of dominance. As soon as he retracts his hand, I get the urge to wipe my fingers on my sweatshirt. This may sound strange, but Ty's rough, calloused fingers seem so perfect to me, so real, so raw. This man's fingers are flat and empty; there are no life lines, and I'd be surprised if he even had fingerprints they're so blank. I don't like that, not one, little bit. Besides, he has big, square teeth that are faker than a pair of press on nails, and his hair is greased back, sandy blonde and obviously the product of a very expensive dye job.

Danny is handsome underneath his raunchy aftershave and horrible veneers, but his soul, while not tortured, is far darker than either Ty's or mine could ever be. I didn't examine him last we met, but I was not impressed. Now, I am horrified. Beth cannot marry this man, child or no. I need to separate her from him, but I don't know how to do that without distancing myself from her. This is a sensitive situation, and I am not a very sensitive person. *Crap.*

Beth puts her hand around Danny's bicep and I see a diamond ring glinting on her finger. *When the fuck did that happen? Shit.*

"Oh, you ... " I begin and point. Ty wraps his arms around my waist, possessively, protectively. I both like it and hate it. I wouldn't change it for the world. Beth grimaces but tries to smile, flashing the rock in the poor lighting of the foyer. Noah Scott and Zella Regali watch silently from the archway to the living room. In the background, I hear the *Nightmare Before Christmas* playing softly on the TV.

"I'm just trying it on," she says, but in her voice, I hear a hundred girls crying out for help, asking why somebody didn't take the initiative, the hard path, break them off from the devil and send them on their way. *Why me? Why does it have to be me?*

"Good," I say and try to smile to lighten my words a bit. "Because this is definitely something that Jade and India are going to want to talk about with you." Danny watches me carefully, pale blue eyes as cold as an arctic glacier. This is the kind of man that hits his wife without any idea of the mental pain he's causing her, who relishes that physical crack and thinks he's in the right because he *owns* her. This is a man that will terrify Maple, who will keep her down and questioning, who will install the very framework that could lead to the life I've led. I want to just say what I think outright, but I can't. This man is rich and probably powerful because who am I kidding, in this strange, strange world we all live in, one often goes hand in hand with the other. "They're not ready to lose their mother yet," I say and Danny laughs. It's not a pleasant laugh. I think, but I'm not sure, that Ty growls softly in my ear. Wherever McCabe is right now, it is not in this room. Mr. McCabe is somewhere else altogether, in another time, another place. Not good. I need to remove him from the situation before things go downhill and end up putting us all in an even worse frame of mind than we are now. After all, this is a time of fresh starts and healing, and I cannot lose sight of that.

"I think Jade and India are old enough to start living their own lives and letting poor Beth find her own happiness."

"I agree," I say and continue before Danny's grin of triumph can send me into a rage. It's been awhile, but I've always been prone to rages. I once smashed a girl's head against a stage at a concert because she elbowed me. "But I don't think her happiness is with you."

"Excuse me?" he asks, stepping forward, rather aggressively. In my head, I go back to dog analogies again. Dogs are so simple and so straight fucking forward. They tell you the way it is and they don't bullshit. Man's best friend. Never were truer word spoken. When I get home, I am definitely getting a dog. Can't have a baby in the dorms anymore than you can have a dog. I'll have to find somewhere else to live, preferably with Ty by my side.

"Never," Beth admonishes, but she seems almost relieved. That really freaks me out. If Beth is beyond the point of scolding me, then she's in a bad place. I can't help but wonder where and when this newest baby was conceived, and then I get this really sick feeling in my belly and I know that this sickness isn't from my baby but rather from my disgust at Danny.

"I think you should go," I tell Danny and that should be that. If he was a good man or even an okay man, he would understand how family dynamics work and he would know that even if Beth was his soul mate, that her girls need time to adjust. He would nod his head slowly, kiss her cheek, and wave goodbye with a *Merry Christmas.* Danny ... wow. Danny proves himself rotten to the core by getting in my face.

"I have a right to spend Christmas Eve with my family," he says indignantly, pointing over at poor Darla who isn't even his child. Obviously, Maple is not his real priority here, not truly. His priority is to claim and own. He wants to see Beth submit to him. *Think dog,* I tell myself as I meet Danny's eyes challengingly and wait for him to spring at me, to tear at my throat with metaphorical teeth. "You've been back, what, a few weeks? And you think you have the authority to tell *me* what to do?"

"Excuse me," Noah Scott says from the sidelines, but I'm not Noah's concern anymore. I'm Ty's, and he's just gone off the deep end.

Without a word, McCabe releases me, steps forward, and decks Daniel Delphino aka Danny square in the face.

5

Ty strips off his shirt and steps into the hot water of the shower with a hiss. While I can't deny that he kicked the shit out of Danny Delphino, he didn't escape unscathed.

"You want a raw steak or something to throw on that shiner?" I ask as I lean against the shower door with my shoulder and try not to stare at Ty's rock hard ass glistening with moisture and shrouded with steam. *Remember to breathe, Never.* I tear my gaze away from his body and try to focus on his face as he turns to look at me, letting the water run through his hair and down his face. Ty isn't looking at me, and he isn't answering. In fact, he didn't speak the whole time he was beating the shit out of Danny nor did he say a word after when Noah and I managed to pry the two men apart. Suffice it to say, Beth was not pleased, but Jade was, and India, too, I think. When they came out of their rooms to check on the commotion and saw what was happening, neither of them moved. Jade gazed down with undisguised glee on her face, and India watched with a hopeful but guarded expression. Beth just cried. I slam the butt of my hand into the door and Ty cringes when it shakes. "I had things under control."

"Did you?" he asks and then he cringes again and turns away from me, grabbing a bottle of shampoo and lathering up his dark, dark hair that glitters like friggin' ebony when its wet. "He was getting tough with you, Nev."

"So?" I ask, refusing to admit to myself how nice it was to see Ty's ringed fingers smash into Danny's perfect jaw. Pretty sure he's going to need Botox or some shit to fix that up. "When have I ever needed you to protect me? I am capable of taking care of myself, you know."

"Maybe, but ... " Ty begins and just stops talking. He's done talking anyway. Before I know what's happening, Ty has my wrist in hand and is pulling me fully clothed into the steam of the shower, slamming my back against the tile wall and kissing the hell out of me. I lift my hands to push against his chest and come across hard, soapy muscles that make my whole body sag like I've just downed a bottle of muscle relaxers. *Wow.* "You're my wife to be. I had to step in there. I'd expect you to do the same for me." I wrap my arms around Ty's neck and let him kiss my ears, my jawline, my throat.

"That's why you attacked him?" I ask and then follow that serious question up with a moan.

"Yup."

"That's the only reason?" We both know that it's not, and I'm just waiting for Ty to lie to me, to prove that we're both the same, that I'm not the only one that can make a mistake. Ty pauses his kisses and puts one hand on the wall above my shoulder. The other slides up my side under my soggy sweatshirt, looking for the quickest, easiest way to get it off.

"I'm a whole barrel of reasons, Nev, but I don't want to talk about them." He pauses and then gives up and uses both hands to tear off the sweater unceremoniously, tossing it out the shower doors and slamming them behind him. "I just want to fuck you and have a very, merry Christmas." I smile, but the expression is tight. There is so much going on inside Ty's head that it's scary. One phone call is changing everything, and I don't like that. My lover boy is like a ball of yarn, ready to unravel, to roll across the carpet and unwind until he's nothing at all anymore but a tangled mess. I cannot let that happen.

"Something about your mother, obviously," I say, trying to prompt him into a story, but only if he's ready. If he's not ready then I'm just going to have to wait because to force Ty to open himself up to me when he isn't ready is like asking him to commit emotional suicide, and if I can't live in this world with Ty fucking McCabe by my side, damaged but perfect, then I'd rather throw myself into the sea. Ty stares at me, and he looks pissed, but his hands are massaging my breasts through the white lace of my bra, so I know he's not about to lose it completely. I can still push him a little.

"Should we ... should *I* leave tonight? Let you spend Christmas with your sisters and just get this over with? I don't want you to miss out on presents and shit because the bitch decides to up and die on the worst day of the year. She was always like that, selfish. You know?"

"No, I don't know," I say and Ty stops massaging my breasts. Not good. "Because you never tell me. I don't know anything about your mother except that you stole her rings and that she ran over your cousin with her SUV." I huff, but I'm not angry at Ty, not really, just at the circumstances of our lives and how fucked up they are.

"She also liked to photograph cars and keep her son in a house with a twice accused child molester, so there's that, too." He is full on frowning now, standing there soapy and naked and wet and miserable. I don't know if it's because he's really worried about his mom or if he really does hate her as much as he says, but I know I only have one choice in the matter and that is to calm Ty down. He's been guiding me since that day he took me to the clinic and to SOG, and now he needs help. I imagine another dog reference and am surprised at how much that simple idea calms me. *Take control of the leash and when he's calm, reward him.*

"Ty," I begin and he takes my face in his hands and kisses me gently on the lips, nipping lightly with his teeth when he pulls back. It's a weird kiss, like a goodbye or something, and it really freaks me out, so I reach around him and grab hold for dear fucking life. "If you leave without me, I will hunt you down and castrate you." Ty chuckles, but I'm not done. "And if you leave without opening presents with my sisters, they will collectively hunt you down and kick your ass, so don't suggest it again, you're staying."

"Beth might be pissed," he begins, but I reach down and wrap my hand around his surprisingly erect cock. *See, stud. I told you. Even ticked off, he's ready and rearing to go.*

"Beth will be fine," I promise as I use the slippery lather of the shampoo to run my hand back and forth along Ty's shaft, feeling with my fingers, exploring, caressing. We don't do stuff like this often, so it's nice. I'm getting to know Ty's body in a way I've never known anyone else's. I like that. "Now shut the fuck up and kiss me," I say and Ty makes a small clicking sound in the back of his throat.

"Not until – " he begins, and I'm forced to increase the strength of my grip until he moans and presses into me, wrapping his long fingers around my biceps as he sucks in a massive breath and lets his head fall back. "Just say it," he groans, and since I don't know what he's talking about, I continue my journey, stepping in and running my fingers through his hair, pulling his face to mine and kissing him hard and fierce.

"Say what?" I ask as Ty's eyelids flicker closed and his breathing relaxes into a slow, heavy pant.

"Fuck Noah Scott," he whispers as the muscles in his arms and shoulders tense and he gives fully into the pleasure of my hand, the touch of my lips as I press them into the hollow of his throat. "Say it."

"Fuck Noah Scott," I tell him and mean it.

6

Later that night, I wake to find Ty missing from bed, leaving this warm, empty place where his body had been resting. It's a strange feeling for me to process, but the thought that I now have a 'side' of the bed makes me unbelievably happy while at the same time, I stress because I am so positive that Ty McCabe has run away that by the time I find him smoking on the porch, I have tears in my eyes.

He's shirtless and pretty standing in the bright moonlight

that reflects off the snow like a mirror, highlighting the bright butterflies on his hands and arm, turning them neon, spots of color against all of that white. When he hears the screen door, Ty McCabe turns around and finds me with wet cheeks and puffy eyes.

"Babe," is all he says as he opens his arm and I step into it, comforted by the smell of cigarette smoke and the faint glow of the cherry. Ty drapes himself over me and rests his hand on the porch railing, cig clutched between two fingers. His bracelets are missing so all is strangely quiet when he lifts his smoke up to his mouth for a drag. I miss them already.

"Thought you'd run away," I say because guys like Ty, well, that's what they do. When he smiles sadly, eyes locked onto the far away and the has been, the past and the positively painful future, I know that I'm still living with that old cloak of shame and doubt draped over my shoulders. Ty is not the same type of man that he once was, and I'm not the same type of woman. We have both come a long way in a short while, and I need to remember that.

"I'm tired of running," Ty says as he passes the cigarette to me and draws another out of his pocket. I raise it to my lips, but I don't smoke it, just brush it along my mouth until I'm salivating and my heart is pumping a hundred miles an hour. Addiction. It's the second most powerful emotion there is. There's only one that can trump it, and that, that is love. I close my eyes and try to feel Ty's presence, his warmth, his belief that we are worth more in one another's eyes than we were in our own. Love. Love. Love. The only emotion that ranks first in both the pain and pleasure categories on the tumultuous scale of human feeling, the only one that can both start wars and end them, that can kill but that can also make new life. I touch my fingers to my belly and know that this is a good time to tell Ty about our baby. "I guess to move forward, I have to go back?" he asks and I nod.

"Sometimes, the only way to go forward, is to take a few, careful steps back," I say, echoing the very lesson that Ty taught me before with his patience, his confidence, and his trust. "There's something I want ... " I pause because the words aren't right and they need to be. They need to be just right. "No, something that I *need* to tell you," I say and the change in Ty is immediate. Behind me, he tenses and his cigarette falls from his hands, tumbles end over end and hits the snow with a hiss. Ty curses and moves away from me, leaving me shivering in the icy cold starlight. "Ty?" I ask as he moves down the steps and into the snow barefoot, retrieves the cig and comes back with a frown on his face.

"What?" he asks and his demeanor is completely different from before, like he's just turned a 180, gone off in the opposite direction and lost touch with reality. *What the hell?* I shift my feet nervously as I look at him and notice that my cigarette has burned down to a dangerous nub. I deposit it into the ashtray next to the porch swing and try to convince myself that there will be no better time than *now* to tell Ty. If I keep waiting for a certain ambiance, a certain facial expression, a specific tone of voice from Ty, then I might be waiting a long, long while. The past few weeks, he's been perfect, but then, he's been focusing on me and my problems, not on his, and despite his calm, quiet strength and reassuring attitude, he has a lot of them. Maybe living vicariously through me has cured some but not all. There are things living inside of Ty that even I don't understand. After all, I never worked as a prostitute, never saw my worth in dollar signs and making ends meet. I'm not saying that I'm any better or any less damaged than Ty, only that I don't always understand what he's thinking or why. What I can say and that I do know for sure is that Ty McCabe has not gotten snippy with me in a while, and I know, know,

know that at least ninety percent of his attitude is because of his mother. I have to remember that, so I can work gingerly with him, take him under my wing and show him the same love and consideration that he showed me.

"Sit down with me?" I ask as I hold out my hand to indicate the porch swing. Ty looks at it and then at me, and he stares for a long time, eyes shadowed by his position against the moon. I can't see what he's thinking and it makes me nervous. He smiles but there are no dimples, and shakes his head.

"My feet are cold. Let's go back to bed." Ty holds out his hand and I take it though I don't move. Instead of him pulling me forward, I hold him back and try to look him straight in the face. Once again, like a frightened dog, he won't look at me, turning this way and that like he doesn't want to hear what I have t say.

"Ty, I'm – "

"Never," he interrupts and he moves forward, lifting both of his hands so he can take my face between them, kiss my lips with hot fire and draw me into his dark orbit. "I am on overload already, baby. I'm not thinking clearly. I know that, and I'm not afraid to admit it, but whatever you have to say, I won't be able to take it seriously if you tell me now. Can it wait?" My stomach spins and flips and turns over, almost like that bit of Ty that's inside of me is as anxious as he is. I pull away from him and he chases after me, like he thinks I'm trying to run. When I stop at the toilet and throw up Beth's over salted Christmas dinner, Ty breathes a sigh of relief and slumps to the floor in the hallway. "I'm so sorry, Never," he says, and it almost sounds like he's apologizing for something other than his attitude, like he knows. Like he knows. He knows. I pause and raise my head up, turn slowly to find my lover's head back and his eyes closed.

Ty McCabe knows. He has to know. My eyes widen and I'm glad his are closed because if he saw this expression, he'd know that I was onto him. *You fucking idiot, Never,* I think to myself as I swallow hard and flush the toilet to keep Ty from hearing any sounds that may or may not escape my throat. When did he find out? How does he know? Did Beth tell him? I don't know, but at least things make sense now. His wanting to quit smoking, his refusal to hear what I had to say, his proposal …

Fuck.

His proposal.

I turn back to Ty and see that he's not paying attention to me. He is all up in his head, so buried in that shit that he can barely see what's right in front of him. Normally, the man has little to no difficulty reading me like an open book. As of right now, the book is closed and sitting shelved. Ty McCabe is thinking about his mother and his childhood and his dead cousin and his clients and whatever else it was that made him he way he was. He does not see the look of pain and anger that flashes across my expression as he glances up at me and smiles sadly.

"Get me through this?" he asks, and the plea is too genuine for me to ignore. On shaking hands, I crawl across the floor, touch my fingers to the purple bruise around Ty's dark eye and slump against him. He tugs me against him nice and tight, rings digging into my arm while my hands lay limp in his lap and the blue ring glints at me like a warning.

Did Ty McCabe ask me to marry him because he wanted me or because he knew I was pregnant? I won't know until I ask him, but I can't ask him until he lets me. Right now, Ty is shutdown. If I press the point that he so obviously does not want me to bring up, then I'll only be asking for heartache.

"Of course," I say to him and then silently, I add, *and then after, I'll find out what you know and how, what your intentions are and how you really feel.* Ty McCabe loves me, but love alone does not a child raise. I have to figure out what's going on, so I can make some decisions. Tough ones. After all, that's what life's about: hard choices and the way we deal with them.

I promise then and there to prove myself not just to Ty, not just to this baby, not just to this family, but to a person long neglected who is overdue for a bit of respect: myself.

7

I wake on Christmas morning to the sounds of children shouting downstairs, racing up and down the halls, pounding on doors and begging India, Jade, and me to get our butts up. Ty is already gone, but on his pillow sits a small box wrapped in silver paper. It's topped with a green bow and there's a small note tucked underneath. I pick this up with a smile, my mind clogged with the happy feelings of sex and sleep, both of which I got in droves last night, and then remember that Ty knows. Ty knows that I'm pregnant but hasn't said a thing, so he's lying to me, too, in a way. I frown and unfold the note.

The words are in Ty's handwriting, small and scrawled, heavy and dotted with ink splotches because he presses too hard when he writes. Ty tells me he's broken his fair share of pens in his life, and I believe him. I read the words carefully, searching for McCabe's true feelings for me in the text.

Never, it begins with a carefully placed date and time in the upper right hand corner. *I'm no Noah Scott in the poetry department, but I know you like guys with words of their own, so here it goes. P.S. If you make fun of me for this, I'll never forgive you. xxxOxxx Ty.*

I peel the top page of the note back and tuck it behind the bottom.

Untitled Poem for the Love of my Fucking Life
by Tyson Monroe McCabe

Roses are red
Violets are blue
Never Ross, I heart the fuck out of you.

I snort with laughter as I reread the three simple lines that Ty has penned for me and decorated with flourishes. There are swirls, hearts, lips and even a few naughty bits drawn with careful precision. *Now open your fucking gift,* it says on the bottom. I fold the page up and know that although Ty is not a master manipulator of the English language, that his poem is my favorite if only because he wrote it. *Sorry Noah,* I think as I put the box in my lap, untie the ribbon and find a dog collar.

"Shit," I say, but already there's a smile on my face. "Shit, fuck, Ty McCabe," I say as I swing my feet out of bed and fight back a wave of nausea. *Look at me,* I think as I finger the purple and pink polka dotted collar with my fingers. *I'm your all American girl now. I've got a fiance, a baby, and a dog. Goddamn.* I finally give into my nausea and head to the bathroom, but I don't stay long. I have to see what my tatted bad boy has done, what stupid decision he made based on a few choice words from me. At least it's proof that he listens to what I say. I've only told him about my wishes for a dog offhandedly, and it certainly isn't anything we've talked about. Somehow though, Ty knows. Ty always knows.

I put some slippers on my feet, check to make sure my hair isn't too terribly mussy, and head down the stairs to find bitch-Never playing with a gray and white pit bull. Noah and Ty both supervise from the archways to the kitchen and living room respectively while the little girls gaze at the new dog with awe and a bit of raw jealousy in their faces.

"Tyson McCabe," I say and my bad boy cringes, switching his gaze over to me with a guilty expression of pleasure turning up the corners of his sexy lips. "What on earth have you done?"

"You said you wanted a dog," he tells me with a gentle shrug, and I have to avoid Noah's eyes because he's looking at me with *something* that I don't like. Zella comes out of the kitchen and he moves aside to let her pass, but the way she looks at him and the way he's looking at me, I know she's told him. I try not to let a frown grace my mouth and move down the stairs so that the dog – *my* dog – can sniff my crotch.

"I live in the dorms," I say, but I want to be happy, so I just am. I follow the wagging tails of the two dogs as an example and just live in the moment, just feel for a second the way I want to feel. I will worry about Noah and Zella and the baby and Ty and his mother later. Right now, I'm bending down and getting a face full of slobber as I hook the collar around my new friend's neck.

"Adoption fee's nonrefundable," Ty says with a silly wink. "Plus, she's a real good, bitch. Kind of like you." I flip him off and the little girls *ooh* at our dirty display. Beth comes out of the kitchen at the perfectly wrong moment and gives me a *look*.

"No fingers in front of the kids, Never," she tells me, proving with a few, simple words that she is no longer angry at Ty; she doesn't correct him. I also notice that the engagement ring is no longer on her finger, and I can't help but wonder what happened between her and Danny. I'm afraid to ask. I'm even more afraid of what will happen when I leave with Ty today, how she'll react to my departure and how she'll behave when I'm gone. I'm not particularly into controlling the sex lives of others, but I know I don't want Beth with Danny. I have to protect her from the pain he could cause. I just have to. Beth deserves better.

"What's her name?" Lorri asks me, tugging on the sleeve of my oversized white tee, the one that I borrowed from Ty. I look up at the man in question and he shrugs at me.

"Your dog," he says as he slips a cig between his lips and gets a dirty look from Beth. I sigh and sit down, crossing my legs and thinking about how this gray dog and I are a match made in heaven. She's a pit bull: one of the most misunderstood creatures on the planet. No doubt she's had to overcome obstacles to be here in my arms, and I don't doubt that she'll experience many more, that people will judge her based on what she is and not who she is. That's tough. I let her kiss my face and try to think around her slobber and bitch-Never's high pitched barking that Noah is always hard-pressed to put a stop to.

Ty watches me carefully as I think about this dog's name and how hard it is to pick just one word, one descriptor, one something to help define who she is, where she's been and what she'll become. *Think this is hard? What about naming a baby?* I swallow a painful lump and push that thought back. *Live in the now because the now is all you're guaranteed to have. The future is a far off concept, something that may or may not happen. You don't have to ignore it, but you don't have to obsess about it either.*

"Well," I begin as I hear footsteps and glance over my shoulder to find India and Jade both coming down the stairs. Maple and Darla are sitting on the floor near Ty's feet while Lettie and Lorri pet the dogs beside me; Beth watches; Ty watches; Noah watches with Zella's eyes sliding back to his face every now and again. There is only one person who should be here, but is not. "You know how recycling is good for the earth?" I speak slowly, so that they can all hear me. "How you can take something that's used, that's basically garbage, and make it new and fresh again?"

"You want to name her Recycle?" Lorri asks and both she and Lettie laugh. I smile at them, but I continue on, convinced that my decision is the right one. This dog and her name are now symbolic of my life. I have a feeling that we'll be together forever.

"I'm going to name her Angelica," I say, and it takes the younger girls a moment to understand. Beth, however, gets it right away. She tucks her short hair behind her ear and smiles softly at me.

"I like it, Never," she says as we both realize the impact our missing mother has and will continue to make on us both. "What do you think, Ty?" I look over at him and see that he's grinning from ear to ear.

"I think that's fucking perfect."

"Language," Beth says slowly. "Language."

8

We manage to make it through a pancake breakfast and a frenzy of presents, paper, and toys before Ty's decision to leave comes out in the worst way possible – by accident.

"Wait, what?" Beth asks after Ty makes an offhanded comment about *coming back*. He pauses suddenly, like he's frozen and frowns. He's been stroking Angelica's fur for awhile now, and the dog looks like it's in heaven. His bracelets have been tinkling a merry rhythm that's lulled me into a sleepy state where I can barely keep my eyes open. As my sister's hazel eyes slide over to mine, I have no choice but to sit up and take a deep breath.

"Ty's mother is in the hospital," I say as I let my gaze trail over to India, Zella, and Noah. Of course, he's the first one to speak. Noah is good with these types of situations.

"I'm so sorry to hear that," he says as he leans forward and tilts his blonde head to the side, steeples his fingers in front of him and tries not to let his thigh touch Zella's. The poor girl is gunning for him like crazy and I know that she's waiting for the perfect moment to ask me if it's okay, if she can have him, love him the way I could've if I hadn't run away. *If I hadn't found Ty.* I don't let myself have any regrets and resolve to pull her aside before I go. Noah has a right to love someone else, and I want Zella to be happy. Besides, the boy fits into our family like a piece of a puzzle, filling the missing slot that my mom's left unoccupied. Guess we should keep him in the family. "I hope it's not too serious?"

"Actually," Ty says as he sits up tall and blows out a big breath, one that smells like maple syrup and cigarettes. As strange as it sounds, it's actually comforting and it makes me want to kiss him, steal his worries away with my lips, hide them deep down with the rest of mine and lock them away. But then, could we ever really be happy if I did that? Could we ever really start fresh with old memories rotting inside of me, poisoning me from the inside out? I don't think so. "It is. In fact," Ty pauses and glances up at the clock above the fireplace. "The old broad might be dead already." Noah cringes, and I don't blame him. It's hard to hear the way Ty talks about his mother, even if she is a horrible person. I see Beth craning her neck after the little ones, but they're outside in the snow with Jade, so all is good. "That's why I have to go, just in case," Ty tells the sad, sorry faces on the couch kitty-corner from ours. "I have to see her if I can, or I'm never going to get over this ... this *hatred* that I have for her." Ty runs his hands over his face and shakes his head.

Nobody speaks for a moment, so I step in and make sure it's understood that this is not something that Ty and I have been hiding from the family, just something that was sprung on us spur of the moment that we have to deal with.

"Ty got the call yesterday," I begin as I put out a hand and rest it on his knee. My blue engagement ring looks so bright in the glow of the Christmas lights and the warm flicker of the candles on the fireplace mantel. I wish I could stay here, soak up the holiday cheer, and announce to my family Ty's and my union with a glass of champagne that I can't drink. "We didn't want to spoil the morning by telling you ... " I trail off as my sisters' faces fall, and I realize that they didn't know I was going with him.

"You're going, too?" Beth says, and her voice sounds very tight, like she's on the verge of tears. I think she was counting on my being here for the next few weeks. I think my pregnancy is helping her deal with hers, and besides, these past few weeks have been wonderful. I would do anything to stay with my sisters, but Ty needs me now, and I can't let him down. If I let him go without me, he might do or say something that he's going to regret for the rest of his life. I have to protect him, even if he won't acknowledge the secret that's festering between us. I nod, but I have a hard time getting the word *yes* past my tight-lipped frown. I knew I would have to leave eventually, go back to school, and say goodbye to my sisters for a little while. Despite what some people think, texts and phone calls are not the same. Still, I didn't expect it to come so soon or to hit me so hard when it did. Now that the word is out and Ty is nibbling his lip ring anxiously, I know it's time to go and my heart starts beating fiercely, begging me to stay.

"How are you going to get there?" Noah asks, and he's not being rude, just curious. Already, I see wheels and cogs turning in his blue eyes while he examines the two of us and calculates our resources. They are few and far between to be certain, and I know he's about to make us an offer, one that I hope doesn't offend Ty.

"I was hoping we could catch a bus," Ty says as he glances at the clock for the second time. His ringed fingers are now tapping a steady rhythm on the arm of the couch nervously. I think for a while there, he'd forgotten all about his mother, got caught up in the laughter and the shouting and the presents. Now that the little girls are outside and both dogs are resting quietly on the floor, he's remembered the unpleasant task that lies before us. What exactly will happen when we arrive at his mother's bedside is beyond me, but I know that it isn't going to be a cherished memory for any of us. "I checked the schedule. There's one that runs today, but it leaves at noon, so we should probably get ready to go."

"I could get you some plane tickets," Noah blurts, and I have to force myself to look at his face, at his desperation. He wants to make me happy even if he can't have me. It's one of the worst things I've ever seen, and I feel horrible about it. *I really hope Zella can make him happy.* "Not many people fly on Christmas, so it should be pretty easy to get you some seats. I could even drive you to the airport." I look over at Ty and try to see if he's offended, if he's one of those people who throw up their hands in the face of generosity and say, *I don't take handouts!* or something as equally ridiculous. Instead, he looks relieved, grateful even.

"Thanks man," he says with a sigh of relief. "I can't even tell how you amazing that would be." Ty pauses. "It might be awhile before I can pay you back." Noah smiles and he looks very angelic and pretty with his blue plaid sweater, tender eyes, and blonde hair that glows like a halo in the living room light. Zella is gazing at him with unbridled affection, and I can't help but wonder how deep their relationship really goes. Have they slept together? I shake my head. It's none of my damn business.

"Merry Christmas," Noah says as he stands up and pulls his phone out of his back pocket. "This is a gift to you both. No worries."

"Are you coming back after?" Zella asks and Ty nods, slapping his hands on his thighs.

"That's the plan," he says. I don't bother to tell him that things don't always go according to plan. After all, the best laid schemes of mice and men often go awry.

9

I pack all of my stuff because I don't know what's going to happen. I notice that Ty does the same, but I don't mention it. The only question I do have is about the dog, but Noah answers that as soon as I come out of the bedroom with my bag and find Lettie and Lorri crying on the bottom step.

"I'll take Angelica with me for now," Noah says, and I nod, already upset at the idea of being separated from the dog. I may have only known her for hours, but I like her. She's happy go lucky and just damn proud to be alive. I think we all could learn a lot from our new four legged friend.

"Thanks," I say as I notice Ty frowning. I have a feeling he got the dog before he got the phone call from his mother's lawyer. The logistics of Angelica's acquisition are a mystery to me, but however Ty went about it, I'm glad. *How is it that Ty's always two steps ahead of me?* I wonder to myself as I descend the stairs and find myself trapped between two babbling young girls. They don't want me to leave anymore than I want to go. When Ty passes by me, he won't even look at me. Somehow, he's ashamed though I can't say why. To me, it feels like the most natural thing in the world to go with him. I'm going to have to show him how worth it he really is.

"I didn't know if you had a hotel in mind … " Noah begins and then swallows, avoiding my eyes and locking his gaze on Ty. His face says he both respects and envies the man, but he doesn't hate him. *Oh how mature you are, Noah Scott,* I think as I watch him and know that he would have made a great husband. His only problem would've been that he wasn't Ty, and that, that was a deal killer. "So I booked one for you, just in case."

"Thank you," Ty whispers, obviously relieved. I don't know where he had planned on staying, but wherever it was, he's relieved that he doesn't have to go there. "One day, I'll pay you back."

"Sure," Noah says, but he doesn't care, not really, and not just because he's rich, just because he's Noah Scott. His heart is as pure as hearts can be, and all he wants to do is help. This reminds me of something, so I pry myself away from Lettie and Lorri with a promise that I will be back before they even realize I'm gone and pull Zella aside. Beth must assume that I'm going to say something about my baby, so she keeps the little ones away from us.

I take Zella down the hallway and out the back door, doing my best not to smile wickedly at the tractor as the screen closes behind us.

"Zella," I say before she can say a single word. I turn her to face me and stare into her eyes, find the flecks of green that mirror mine and smile. Zella is so pretty, and fortunately for her, she looks more like our late father than she does our evanescent mother. "I wanted to pull you aside and let you know ... " *How to say this, how to give up ownership of a man that was never really mine ...* "That I think you and Noah make a cute couple." Zella blinks at me for a long while and then glances away like she's ashamed, tucking some of her brunette hair behind her ear.

"Am I that obvious?" she asks, and I have to bite my lip to keep from laughing. I touch her chin and turn her to face me again. I don't want her to feel bad about this. I have no right to make her feel like that. I have Ty's ring on my finger, his baby in my belly, and most importantly, his heart in my chest.

"Nah," I say even though that's a lie. It's a white one though, one that shines, that lights up Zella's face and makes her smile.

"I'm so sorry, Nev. I never intended to take him from you, and I came back thinking that he was off limits, but then I saw you with Ty and then I found out you were pregnant and ... " She pauses and takes a big breath, stopping herself before she can go off on a tangent. She leans forward and takes me in her arms instead and breathes a heavy sigh as she holds me tight. "Be careful," is all she says. "Don't let him burn you." When she pulls back, there's this ... this *something* in her face that says that someone has done exactly that to her. My big sister instincts take over, and I want nothing more than to delve into the past few years that I've missed and catch up on Zella's heartbreak. Texas is just a hop, skip and a jump away. There's always time for me to head over there and castrate some bastards.

"I won't," I promise, thinking of how easily Ty could crush me if he wanted. Ty has my bloody, beating heart in the palm of his hand, and it's naked and bare for him. I am slowly taking down all my shields, leaving myself open for attack, but I trust Ty, I do. I trust him to hold my tortured soul in his ringed hand and breathe nothing but love and life and happiness into it. "And I love you."

"I love you, too," she replies, and we part, not forever, not this time. This time I fully intend on coming back, of keeping touch, and that makes all the difference. Zella is getting teary, but I refuse to do so because there are so many better things to cry about. I save them for later, somehow certain that I'm going to need them in the next few days, the next few days in which Ty's limits will be tested and my newfound strength will be, too. He's supported me through my fears, stabbed that little monster inside of me with his sharp wit, and I think that finally, *finally* the real me is waking back up. I may even have to dance for him, but I'm not going to mention it, not yet, not until this whole baby thing has been discussed.

"I better get going," I say and she nods, but she doesn't follow me back inside. Instead, she turns away and gazes out across the snowy field, obviously lost in thought. I wonder if Noah will write poems for her or if I've killed something inside of him. I hope not because I'd be awfully sad if I never got another piece of Noah Scott poetry. Ty is great, but a poet he is not.

When I go back inside, Noah is waiting with my suitcase in his hand, but Ty is nowhere to be seen.

"He's having a smoke," he tells me as he searches my face for information. There's nobody in this foyer now except for us and the dogs. My family has never been great with goodbyes which is possibly one of the reasons I left and never looked back. If we had been good with that sort of thing, then maybe I'd have told someone, maybe a cheery goodbye would've changed my mind? I shake my head because honestly, it really is time for me to stop going down that path, to stop thinking about what might have been and start loving what's happening now.

"Sounds like Ty," I say, and I'm trying to be lighthearted and silly, but Noah isn't feeling my mood. His pale cheeks are red and his lips are cracked; he can't seem to stop running his tongue across them. I stare at him, and he stares back at me.

"About what I said ... " he begins. I cut him off. He has to feel good about what he did because otherwise, he will never move on. If Noah can't let go of me now, he will be stuck the same way we've all been stuck these past few years. I love him and even though it isn't the same love I feel for Ty, I can't stand to see him suffer. I need to push him up and over this hump, so that he can be happy whether it's with Zella or not.

"I'm pregnant with Ty's baby, and he knows," I say and Noah blinks like he's in shock. "He knows, but I haven't told him. I tried to tell him today, but he wouldn't let me. From a guy's point of view, tell me, what does that mean?" Noah takes a big breath and sets my suitcase on the floor, glancing over his shoulder like he thinks Ty might come storming in here at any moment. He won't though. Ty is too caught up in his imagination, dreaming up scenarios of what will happen with his mother, what she might say, what he wants to say. I know that because I went through the very same thing on the way here, sitting on that bus wrapped in doubt and old pain with nothing but Ty to keep me going. Nothing but beautiful, tortured Ty.

Noah takes my shoulders in his hands and makes me look at him. Almost instantaneously, he has shifted from scorned lover to concerned friend. How, I don't know, but why I understand perfectly. Noah is a one of a kind guy – no, human being. Noah is a one of a kind human being who actually puts others before himself. We could all learn a lot from tasting just a little bit of the world's Noah Scotts. Anyhow, I think he has practice. After all, he's been communicating with Zella all these years. Noah has gotten really, really good at advice.

"From a lover's point of view," Noah begins. "And not just a man's, I think that Ty is just scared. He wants you, Never." Noah closes his eyes and his blonde lashes flutter like butterflies. When he opens them, his gaze is sharp and cutting, drilling a hole right through my doubts and making things seem so clear that I can hardly breathe. "I can see it in his face and it's mirrored perfectly in yours. Love, need, want, whatever. I couldn't have separated you two if I'd tried." I laugh and shake my head.

"You're saying you didn't?" I begin and Noah laughs, too, and there's this sudden release of energy into the world, like the two of us were holding on to a part of the powers that be and twisting them together, praying, begging and hoping for one another even though we didn't really belong together. Now that we've let it go, I feel lighter, brighter, and the world seems like it's spinning just a bit better, less crookedly; I can finally see straight.

"Okay," he admits reluctantly. "I did, but I shouldn't have."

"Why?" I ask as he steps back and rubs at his chin thoughtfully. Noah looks up at me, and his face is totally serious when he replies.

"Because I knew the first moment I saw you two together."

"Knew what?" Noah smiles and like Ty's dimpled smile, this one is real, but instead of being reflected in his cheeks, it's reflected in his eyes. They crinkle at the edges and make him seem a bit older than he is, a bit wiser, but in a good way, a way that makes him glow like the sun, ancient and powerful and immovable.

"The only thing that can separate the two of you are yourselves."

10

Ty and I are both afraid of flying.

This fact does not come up between us until we're already seated on the plane, in first class mind you, with Ty taking the aisle seat and me at the window. Our hands are clutched together even tighter now than they were on the bus when all that plagued me were fears of rejection and the frowning faces of my sisters. Now, now all I can picture is the plane taking a nosedive into the earth and taking Ty and me and our baby with it, snuffing out any chance we have at a happy life, leaving Ty's soul to wander the earth and mine ... I blink to clear my head. If I let my imagination run wild, it will go rogue and take me down a path I do not want to travel. Apparently, Ty has the same idea.

"What do you think about joining the Mile High Club?" he jokes, but there's a whole lot of sweat on his upper lip and no way in hell he's got a hard on, not right now. In reality, I think sex is the furthest thing from Ty's mind, but I could always be wrong. Guess I'll find out.

"I think that sounds like something that sounds great in theory, but is poor in practice."

"Uh huh," Ty says, and his voice shakes a bit as an announcement comes over the speakers. Neither of us listen. "You're just saying that because you know I'll rock your world, and you won't be able to hold it in. When I'm finished with you, baby, the whole plane will know what's what and who's who on this big ass bird." Ty says the words with all the cockiness in the world, but his throat tenses and he has to really work at swallowing.

"Have you ever been on a plane before?" I ask, trying to remember if Ty has ever said anything about a trip he's taken. But of course, he hasn't. Ty's past is a dark cloud sitting in the beautiful horizon of our future. I need to get through it now before it decides to rain down on our parade. "Because from what I hear, the bathrooms are pretty fucking small."

"No," Ty replies as he bites at his lip ring with nervous ferocity. "And I've never wanted to set foot on one of these friggin' death traps."

"Cool it," I whisper to him as the passengers across the aisle from us stare. Well, to be fair, they were staring anyway. Ty and I don't exactly look like the kind of people who sit in first class. Well, I don't anyway. Ty, if you look at him right, kind of looks like a rock star. Maybe that's why I feel like most of the glares are mine? Or maybe I'm just projecting. Let's be honest here: I am fucking out of my mind with fear.

"Sorry," he whispers as his eyes close and he squeezes my hand so hard his rings dig in painfully. "I just have no clue what I'm doing." I turn my face to look at my lover and I can see that his words have a dual meaning.

Ty McCabe is terrified.

He's not afraid of his mother, not really. I think he's afraid of the person he became because of her, and I think he's absolutely terrified that he'll be that person again. It's my job to remind him that he'll never be, that he's grown too tall to fall into the shadows of the past. Ty and I will be okay. We have to be because I need us to. My soul needs us to; his soul needs us to. This thing between us, this bit of heat that burns like fire, that singes and sears and chars, this is more than just a physical thing, more than just an emotional one, this is a spiritual journey. Neither Ty nor I are religious, and we don't know what happens after death, but we both know that if we die without experiencing the best parts of life, that somehow, we'll be missing out, that the universe in all its infinite glory will be thrown off base somehow.

"Talk to me," I tell him as the plane gets ready to take off, as sounds we've never heard blare from outside, as people strap on their seat belts and plug in their headphones. "Tell me your story." I don't want Ty to hurt himself, but if he's ready, then I need to know.

Brown eyes open and turn to face me. Ty gazes at me with all his darkness and welcomes me in.

11

Okay, so, here's what happened to me, right? It isn't fucking pretty, and I'm not fucking telling you to get your goddamn sympathy. I just ... I guess I just need to let it out now, before I see her because once I do, things will be different between her and me, between you and me, between myself and me. I can't give it all to you at once because there's too much and it hurts me bad to say it, so I'm going to do what I can because I can tell you so desperately need it and because, Never, I love you so much it friggin' hurts inside. I don't think I was built to love this much, to care so much. You stretched me in ways that I cannot explain, and when I look into your face, I see myself reflected there. In your pain, I see my own, so I'm going to tell you and only you, okay? And God, I love the way that you accepted me before and after, that you saw something in me, that you'll still look at me like that when I'm done.

Well, I guess I should start at the beginning because nobody knows the end and the in between, the in between is just too damn hard to talk about right now. Here goes ...

One day, I was born to a woman who didn't love herself and to a man that didn't love her. He was gone before I could even comprehend that he was ever there. I think, at first, she thought he was going to come back, and she was good to me. That didn't last long. Once she realized that I was all she had and that he was never, ever going to love her again, that he wasn't even going to think about her or the son he fucked up without even realizing how or why he was fucking him up, she stopped being a good mom and started being a good fuck, a good date, a good girlfriend, whatever it was that she could be.

You know how some people want to climb the corporate fucking ladder? How they all work their fucking asses off trying to be the CEO? Well, that's what my mom did except she didn't do it at work, and her goal wasn't CEO, it was wife. She just wanted to be a wife. Why? I don't know. Maybe so she could pretend that she valued herself? Maybe so she could say that someone else valued her? Maybe so she never had to work at another strip club again? Whatever the reason, that was her single purpose in life.

Let me rewind real quick, because fuck, Never, I can't tell you about my mom without telling you about my grandma. She was a real good woman, a real good person. My grandma was one of those women that you read about, that change things for those around them and make the world look like it's not just a dump of unwashed bodies and tortured souls. My grandma was the only person that really looked at me and saw Tyson Monroe McCabe and not just that kid or that burden or whatever. But she died because, well, that's what old people do, and for awhile after, Mom was better. I guess in her mother's mortality, she saw her own and so she started taking pictures of cars, really nice ones. The images reflected the person she might have been had she been stronger inside, been capable of caring for us both and not relying on somebody else to do. But, as all weak things are wont to do, that didn't fucking last long ...

Because she met him.

She met the man who changed me from a little boy to a terrified young man, and if he wasn't already dead, trust me, I would kill him ...

12

I blink and suddenly we're up in the air and there are clouds beneath us, white, fluffy clouds that seem less like bits of earth and more like sculptures crafted from the hands of artistic geniuses. Ty has stopped talking and is staring at them, too. There's a can of soda in his armrest that I never saw him ask for and a blank expression on his face that scares the shit out of me.

"What happened to you, Ty?" I ask, and he blinks, too, and then he's grinning at me from ear to ear with the silliest, most ridiculous facial expression I've ever seen. It's fake, too, and lacks his signature dimples, the ones he doesn't really know he has but that make him so easy to read.

"You sure you don't want to fuck?" he asks a tad too loudly and folks stare or maybe they never stopped staring, and I'm just now noticing it. "Because I really want to be the first of my friends to join the MHC." I roll my eyes because I can tell that Ty is done talking. His hands are shaking and his eyes dart this way and that, desperate to see anything but his past. It's like a monster, the one that hides under your bed, that only comes out at night when you're most afraid. This monster stares at Ty and bares its teeth and he cannot, cannot, cannot look at it straight in the face. One day, he'll have to. He'll have to look at it and tell it to fuck off, but for now, he avoids its gaze and stares at my crotch like it's a safe haven, a refuge of some sort. I flick him in the chin and make him look at me. If he isn't ready for his monsters, that's okay, because I'm here and I'm willing to fight for him; I will *always* be willing to fight for him and that, that is a fact of life, love and happiness.

"You cannot use sex as an escape," I tell him although he already knows that. Ty nods his head and reaches for my left hand.

"I know that," he whispers softly, grabbing my sea blue ring, the one that somehow has come to symbolize our love, and sliding it off my middle finger, slipping it gently down to its rightful place on my ring finger. The gesture makes my chest tight and my heart thump painfully. "But with you, it's not like that. It's not like I'm escaping, it's like I'm already in friggin' paradise." I snort with laughter and Ty smiles, leaning over to sear my mouth with a hot kiss, one that burns so fierce that it almost hurts.

"What a line," I say as I shake my head. "What a fucking line." I pause. "If we get caught then it's all on you. I'll tell the air marshal that you blackmailed me into it." Ty grins like a madman and claps his hands together, garnering yet another set of fresh stares from suits and trust fund kids, executives and lucky folks who think that money grows on trees.

"You see," he tells me with all due seriousness, rubbing his strong jaw with long fingers. "This is why I love you so damn much."

"Go to hell," I tell him as he stands up and moves over to the bathroom, a sight for sore eyes in his tight, black jeans, brown boots, and bright, red tee. Getting through security with him was not easy. *Prejudice fucks.* I watch Ty drift down the aisle slowly, and I'm pretty damn sure that's he flashing me his ass on purpose just to get me in the mood. Either that or it's a distraction technique. I close my eyes for a moment and try to process the start of Ty's story. It wasn't much, but at least he's trying to pry himself open, to let me in, to give me the chance to judge his tortured soul. I already know beyond a shadow of a doubt that I'm going to give it my seal of approval, whatever that's worth. It doesn't matter if Ty's mother makes mine seem like Martha fucking Stewart or if he worked the corner, if he gave ten dollar hand jobs or screwed girls for petty cash. Those events are just unfortunate circumstances strung together, obstacles placed before Ty, so that he could become the strong, selfless human being that he's evolved into.

I open my eyes and see that Ty is waiting outside one of the bathroom doors with a smirk on his face, a hot, sharp slash that warms up the air around me, heated by my own feelings and the ardor that's totally inappropriate and absolutely inescapable.

Ty enters the bathroom, and I turn my head forward, back towards the large, gray seat in front of me, determined not to give myself away by acting too anxiously. After all, I've seen one too many horrible scenarios in movies regarding the infamous Mile High Club. I suppose now I'll get to find out if it's really a reality or if Ty's just shitting with me. I want to erase his pain, though, give him something else to occupy his mind for a little while. After all, he did the same for me on the bus, took something that used to be my weakness, twisted it around so that it was not only a distraction technique but a bonding exercise that drew the two of us together in ways that I can still barely understand. For so, so long, sex was just this *thing,* this dangerous activity with physical and emotional consequences that I ignored in desperation, wildly fighting to fill that emptiness inside of myself. Now, my feelings for Ty and my family sit there and make my heart tight with love, and sex has become ... something else. It's just pleasure and not pain, another way for me to show Ty how I feel and vice versa, a stress reliever, exercise, relaxation ... It's all of those things and more. It's something for him and me alone, just the two of us. Just us. Us, us, us.

I swallow hard and stand up, trailing my fingers along Ty's armrest as I move away from our seats and find the door, open it, and step inside. Well, okay, I don't step inside. I can't really *step* because there's nowhere to step. The bathroom's about half the size of the shower stalls back at the dorms.

"Ty," I say as he sweeps me in and presses me up against the tiny counter with the hard lines of his body. Already, I can feel the stiffness in his pants, needy and hungry for me, desperate to forget. "There's not exactly any room in here for the two of us." Ty smiles wickedly and reaches down between us, making me glad that I'm wearing a skirt. If I'd been wearing pants, this whole charade would've been virtually impossible.

"That's okay," he tells me as his zipper slides down and he pushes my panties aside with his fingers, brushing his calloused skin across my warm heat, making me bite my lower lip to keep quiet. "Because I'm going to be inside of you soon enough. That oughta help with the lack of space."

"Ty," I whisper because he's talking too damn loud and right now, with him pushing against me, I just can't seem to care. I grab my lover's face between my hands, soak in that look in his eyes, that set of his jaw, memorize the glint of the poor bathroom lighting on his eyebrow ring, his lip ring; I study Ty's curved lips, his strong cheekbones and the slight dip of dimples that I cannot even express how glad I am to see. "Promise me something before ... " I gasp and have to close my eyes to keep my groans in check; Ty is sliding into me so wicked slow, and I can feel the hot burn of his gaze raking my face, taking me in, memorizing me the same way I'm memorizing him.

"Anything," Ty whispers against my ear, breath warm as it tickles my skin, slides through my hair like gentle fingers. He grabs my ass with his rough hands, pulls me forward into him so that we're pressed tight, taking advantage of all that tight space to come together, to find solace in one another's arms. When we're like this, Ty and me, it feels like two halves of a broken heart are coming together, clicking into place, starting to beat. Blood flows between the two of us, nurturing, reviving, soothing.

"You said things will change between us after this," I begin and Ty pauses, looking up and over my shoulder into the mirror behind us. I see his own reflection flickering back from the deep chocolate of his eyes. Deep down, Ty is scared, oh so scared. I wrap my arms around him and dig my fingers into the fabric of his T-shirt. "And I understand that. That's okay. Change is good. Even the best things have to change or life gets stale, but promise me that when it comes to us, things will only change for the better."

"God, I love you, baby," he says, but he doesn't say *yes*. He. Doesn't. Say. Yes.

"Ty ... " I begin, but he cuts me off by thrusting hard into me, sliding warm and deep into my very soul. I bite into his shoulder, taste his warm, sweaty flesh between my lips and join the Mile High Club, certainly one of life's finest, fucking achievements. Ty slams his ringed hand into the mirror and it cracks, splits right down the middle with a sound like grating glass.

"Oops," he says, but his eyes are half lidded and heavy. He is halfway between here and there, between the past and the present, loving me but barely registering why. Ty is checking out, but I can't stop him because there's a woman at the door knocking.

"Excuse me," she asks. "Is everything okay in there?" And I have these terrible movie references playing out in my head, warning me that as soon as the door opens, the entire plane will be watching.

"Everything is fine," I say, but my voice sounds breathy and just a bit husky. I kiss Ty's lips, bite his ring, suck it into my mouth and taste hot metal, run my hands up his shirt and find his nipples. Ty is a marathon fucker, as strange as that may sound. I figure it's from all the practice, but I cannot friggin' think like that or I see red, so I just remind myself how good he is, how long he can go, how his rhythm is so in tune with my body. Ty's thrusts match me pulse for pulse as I squeeze around him and forget, if briefly, my mother, his mother, my baby, Noah Scott, the dog, just everything. This is why I was so addicted to sex: it's better than booze at erasing the worries, and it's private. Most people can spot a drunk a mile away, but not a sex addict, never a sex addict.

"Ty," I whisper, trying to keep my vision from spinning, trying to focus on the myriad warning signs and regulation posters that clutter the white, white wall behind the sable haired Butterfly God that fucks like a devil and loves like an angel. "Hurry up."

"Can't," he says, panting, bracelets jingling, body tense and hard.

"We don't have time," I groan though the last thing I want to do is stop. Ty's cock is warm and hard and his body is shuddering against mine, so I hold him tight and fierce and I promise myself that I will never, ever let go.

"Fuck time," Ty whispers as he pauses, grabs my face in both hands and locks gazes so deeply into my black, black soul that I can't find the strength to breathe. "I need you right now, Nev. I need you so, so bad, and I'm sorry. I am so fucking sorry." Ty doesn't tell me what it is that he's sorry for, but I have my guesses. Instead, he tugs my head to his chest and tangles my hair around his ringed fingers. Ty presses us tight, bodies mingling, heating, bleeding pain and sorrow all over one another, so that we're empty of that, so that there's room for other things like love, friendship, forgiveness. Ty comes inside of me, spills more of himself into a place that already belongs to him, as I wrap my legs around him and hold his broken body until the emotion passes and he steps away, cleans us up as best he can, and offers me his hand.

Outside the door, a flight attendant waits with thin set lips and tiny, green eyes in her long, horsey face.

"We have a one person limit for each restroom," she tells us seriously. I glance around the plane but nobody's looking. Somehow, someway, Ty and I have done the silliest, stupidest, most impossible task there is. And I'm not talking about the Mile High Club though in truth, it is kind of impressive. I'm taking about falling in love.

"Got it," Ty says as he pulls me to him and nibbles my ear. "So it's like a monogamous toilet, right? I can deal." I grab my bad boy's hand and pull him away towards his seat, terrified that the giddy glow in his eyes will soon fade to pain.

I hate being right.

13

So Ty and I touch down at the airport which is a big, fucking hullabaloo of screaming children, grumpy parents, and hoity-toity old folks with rolling suitcases and Hawaiian shirts. It's as crowded, cluttered and busy as I'd expected and that's *before* I walked outside and caught a glimpse of the iron and concrete, the steel and glass, that absolute insanity that is New York City. Suddenly, my throat is tight and I can barely breathe. I am so out of my element here. I am a Midwest girl who fled to the Northern bits of California and managed, just barely, to adapt. Now here I am in a place that is so foreign to me that it might as well be another country.

"I'm going to rent a car," Ty tells me as he takes in the slew of yellow cabs, tourists, and this general feeling of *rush, rush, rush* that makes me sick. "The hospital my mom is staying at is actually outside the city limits, closer to Aurora. I doubt we'll able to get a cab to take us all the way there." Ty shrugs and then sighs, rubs the bridge of his nose with his ringed hand. He doesn't want to be here; I don't want to be here. Noah had promised that the airport would be dead on Christmas Day; he was wrong. "Come on."

I follow Ty back inside and we meander over to one of the rental car desks whose line is longer than the Empire State Building is tall, and finally, after much grumbling from McCabe about cost, manage to wrangle ourselves up a very fine midsize sedan whose price tag is so astronomical for a three day rental that I practically have to force my hands to my sides so I don't deck the counter agent. After all, it isn't really her fault.

"Fuck me sideways," Ty grumbles as he tosses our bags in the trunk and looks around, blinking like he's just woken up and found himself in hell. "Christ on a Goddamn, Fucking Cracker."

"Did Noah ... " I begin as I climb into the passenger seat and Ty takes the driver's side. He puts one of his long, long legs in and turns to face me with the keys dangling from his hand and an unhappy look plastered across his pretty lips.

"Noah didn't pay for everything," he says, and then, in typical Ty fashion, tries to turn something that he finds offensive into a joke. "Do you have any idea how much that coffee in the terminal cost me? Makes this fucking car look cheap." He stops talking and sees me looking at him, wondering how the hell he can afford this on a grocery store salary.

"Fucking fuck, Never," he says which is so damn literate I can barely stand it. Ty adjusts his seat to accommodate his tall form. Despite warnings to the contrary, Ty already has a cigarette in his mouth and is lighting up.

"How verbose of you," I say and then immediately regret it. I don't want to fight with Ty, not now, not when he needs me more than ever. Noah's words echo painfully in my skull as I watch the cherry on Ty's cig burn bright against his face, highlighting the curves of those cheekbones, making his skin glimmer with orange light. *The only thing that can separate the two of you are yourselves.* "I'm sorry," I begin though the words are not easy for me to come by. "I just – "

"You just wanted to know if I paid with blood money?" he asks with a sigh as he drops his head and then presses his fingers to his temples. "Which is fine because I did." I swallow hard and try not to show him that somehow, this car now feels dirty to me, like I can't stand to have the upholstery touching my skin. I love Ty and I don't judge him for what he did, but I can't stand thinking about it. He *sold* himself for money; I *sold* myself for brief respites from the pain. Are we really all that different?

"Okay," I say and that's the only word I can get to come out.

"I'm sorry," Ty whispers. "I don't have much money left from … *that,* and I try not to spend it unless I need it, but baby, I already did the dirty deeds, and we need the cash." I look over at him, trying not to frown, happy that he said *we,* but positively certain I don't want to know about those deeds. Want and need are two entirely different things. I reach over and pluck the cigarette from Ty's mouth. His ringed fingers come up immediately and snatch me by the wrist. "Baby, don't," he says, and we just stare at each other, just fucking stare.

Ty's brown eyes look like melted chocolate now, all gooey and formless, like he cannot figure out what he should be feeling or what he wants to feel.

"Why?" I ask as he releases me and sits back, closing his eyes, black eyelashes resting on the pale skin of his face. "I thought we were quitting after?" I try to remember Noah's words from just a few hours prior, how Ty is just scared, and I try to tell myself to wait, that he's not ready, but Goddamn it, I'm scared, too, and I want to say it.

I have your baby inside of me. Help me. I don't know what to do with it. I don't know how to react. Please, please, look at me and say you understand, that you know. Tell me something stupid. Tell me you'll use your whore money to buy a crib and a car and that we can still go to school because we'll make this shit work. Tell me that we'll rent a house and take our dog and we'll both grow up to be good people who raise good people who stop the cycle of abuse in its tracks and make life something beautiful. When I found you, my soul was a barren tree, stripped of its leaves, flowers, stripped of life. When I first met you, you started something; you nurtured me and cherished me and I didn't even know it. Now, I'm ready to blossom and all I need is you to say you understand.

"You've done so damn good," he replies lamely and then cracks a smile. "Wouldn't do anyone any good to stop now, yeah?" I roll my eyes and slam my door, hard. Ty notices, but he doesn't say anything and neither do I. I want to cuss him out, threaten to leave, run off and deal with this myself, but I don't. Ty needs me now more than ever. How could I do that to him?

So instead I sit there in silence and tug at my chip earring, the one that I never take off, that reminds me with each turn of my head that I am a survivor, a survivor of my own, dark heart and my bloody memories. I survived the murder of my father, the betrayal of my family, the loss of my dignity, the depth of my feeling. When I think of things like that, it's hard to stay angry at Ty. After all, my only real problem is that our love has taken root inside of me. Ty has proposed and yes, it might be just because of the baby, but does that matter? I have never been a person who values marriage above all else. Love is love is love; marriage is law and paper.

"I love you," I tell Ty absently, eyes locking onto the window and the scenery that flies by because Ty drives too fast.

"I love you so fucking much," he whispers and his voice is nearly lost in the roar of traffic and the hustle and bustle of the city. I say *nearly* because I will always hear Tyson Monroe McCabe. Whether it's a whisper, a scream, no matter what Ty says, I will always hear him. After all, we're too tangled now to be separated and love, love is a loud thing. It sings for all the world to hear and doesn't care who's listening.

14

Ty has to pull over six times, so that I can freaking throw up. To his credit, he gets out every time and comes over, pulls my hair away from my face and rubs my back. How many bad boys will do that?

"Sorry," I say, and I fight the urge to feed him another lie, to say something stupid like *stomach flu* or *Beth's cooking*. Ty lifts my chin, and I turn my face away, absolutely convinced that no matter how much he loves me, that he does not want to smell my nasty breath.

"Here," he says and hands me a piece of gum which I accept gratefully, trying my best to keep my eyes off of his face. I can't look at him straight right now. Ty McCabe is like a tapestry, and the threads are just starting to come apart. Pull the wrong one and he will go to pieces, slither to the floor in a heap of string and never realize his full potential. I protect him from this by not looking into his eyes or at his face. I focus on his hand instead, on his butterfly tattoos that have always, always fascinated me. "And don't be sorry, this is not your fault." My eyes flicker closed, and I have to do my best to hold back tears. How stupid am I? I want Ty to hold me, to stroke my arm with his long fingers and say that everything will be okay. Naïveté, thy name is Never Ross.

Ty pauses and tucks his hands into his pockets, looks up at the sky and just stares. A gamut of emotions run across his face, a series of events play out behind his eyes, and I know, just know, that as soon as he climbs back in this vehicle, I am going to get part two of Ty's life story. I need to hear it; there's no doubt about that. The thing is, I don't know if I want to anymore. I like Ty the way he is. Do I need to see inside of him? Do I need to see what makes him tick? Will that hurt the beauty that's building between us? It better fucking not.

"Never," Ty begins as he sways in time with the whoosh of cars behind us, caught in this strange in between where the city falls away and the countryside looms. I am beyond glad that we're not staying in the mother of all concrete jungles, that we're leaving and taking our little freak show on the road. "Is it possible to hate *and* love someone at the same time?"

"Yes," I respond without thinking. Thought, sometimes, can be our worst enemy. Now, I'm not saying that it's best to jump in with both feet, not always, but occasionally, you have to suspend your conscious mind or it will fuck you hard and fast and leave you wondering what the hell just happened. I think of Noah's poetry, and I know that I can quote it to Ty without hurting him. After all, Noah Scott will always be a part of me, but now that he is no longer a regret, no longer a threat, it's safe to show that side. "*Broken glass is not always shattered and hollow hearts are not always fractured; There are two sides to every story.*" I tap my hands on my knees. I feel a bit like a hypocrite here, like I'm going to pick apart Noah's poem like that professor in that class that seems so long ago, when Ty brought me coffee and watched the video where my mother ripped out my heart and stomped on it. Which reminds me, I still need to dance for Ty. I want him to have that, to be the last man I've moved for. "To love even though you hate is the greatest accomplish of all. To forgive when you thirst for revenge is the greatest triumph of all." Ty tilts his chin down and watches me carefully, pupils dilating, tongue flicking across his mouth, lips dry and cracked from the dust of the traffic, the grit that flies up and makes me feel skittish about letting the love of my life stand here. "You have to accept that you love what you love, and that's the way it is, even if it makes no sense. Then you release it and let it go." I tell Ty this from experience, thinking of my mother. Ty and I are reflections of the same person, the same life, in different glass, and I love him to fucking pieces.

"I heart the fuck out of you, you know," he says, and I laugh. Ty bends down, grabs my hair roughly, and pulls my mouth against his, burns my words from my throat with his tongue, gives me goosebumps on my neck when he slides his fingers down my skin. Lacey can't stop texting me about pregnant women and how horny some of them are which she thinks is, like, *super cool,* and as annoying as that is, I have to admit, I want nothing more than to push Ty into the back seat and ride him until the sun goes down, comes up and leaves again.

I groan as he pulls away, leaving me warm and wanting, desperate for his touch, his taste.

"Tease," I joke, cheeks flushed, embarrassed at having just kissed a dude after vomiting. How sexy is that? Ty grins, big and wide, but without dimples. I'm starting to miss those fuckers.

"I have to do what I can to keep you around, Never," he says as he moves over to the opposite side of the car. When he climbs in, I tell him the truth.

"You've got me as long as you need me."

15

Thanks for being so patient with me. I know you need to know; I know you gave me everything you had, and I know it's time, but please, wait just a little longer. I have to break this down piece by piece or else this story will break me, tear me up, and toss my remains to the sea. And fuck, Nev, I have just found my reason to live. I have tasted you, and your essence is so much a part of me that if you leave, I will find you, and I will do whatever it takes to keep you. I'm not trying to sound like some creepy fuck, some stalker, or what the fuck ever, but I just know that you and I are meant to be together, alright?

So my mom marries this big, fat, friggin' douche bag who smells like rot, whose smile is like a mouthful of moldy cheese. She marries him because he says he loves her, simple as that. It doesn't matter that it's a lie. My mom might as well be living blind because she no longer sees anything she doesn't feel like seeing – and that includes me.

I watch from the shadows, watch her tie us up in a man who does not understand what it's like to be a part of a family. All he sees is a woman who has inherited some money from her mother, who has a house, and a boy.

Me.

I was just a fucking kid, but he looked at me like he could eat me up, swallow me whole, and make me disappear.

This guy who I refuse to fucking name because he's not worth the monicker, moves into the house my grandma left my mother. Did I ever mention that she wore rings? She picked a different one every day and always had a jewelry box organized by color. She had long fucking fingers, witch fingers I used to call them, but only as a joke. I loved that old broad to pieces.

Right, so mom marries this guy and he moves in, and I know right away that he isn't right. Still, he spends years working up the courage to do what I know he wants to do with me. Every night I prepare myself and I wait for him to come, ready to defend myself.

Until Casey comes.

Casey is my cousin, okay? He's this little, blonde haired, blue eyed dude that looks like Noah probably looked as a brat. Him and me, we looked like angel and devil together. We had fun, too. Serious fun. The kind of fun that only kids can have.

Well, Casey came to live with us because my aunt had

passed away and her husband was missing. I won't go into that. There's a whole story that you don't want to know, a twisted tapestry of deceit, a general fucked-uppedness that will make your head spin. Bad luck sort of follows my family, you know?

Casey comes to live with us and right away, that fat, fucking douche bag is attracted to him. I don't know what happened, Never, but I do know that the day he died, he was a broken kid. I tried to help, really, I did, but I was so young. I...

My mom ran him over with her SUV. She didn't mean to, okay, but she did it because she didn't see what she didn't feel like seeing. That meant Casey and me. That meant the horrible things her husband was doing or wanted to do or whatever. I think on that day, Douche Bag was going to move to the next step. I think Casey ran. I think he was trying to get into the SUV, to stop my mom from leaving us alone with that fucking piece of shit.

That's what I think, but it doesn't really matter because the last thing I noticed about Casey was how sad his eyes were. He died a broken boy, and I was damned if I would be next.

16

Ty and I arrive at the hospital a few hours later, sliding into an empty parking space near the front entrance. Since he finished his story, McCabe hasn't said a word, not one single word. I wrapped my hand around his and held it tight, gazed over at his face and memorized the strong lines of his profile. Ty has nice lips, full and curved, sharp, and at the moment, tense and pursed. They tell stories, those lips, up and down my back, along the inside of my thigh, across the hot heat between my legs. His eyes remain wide and open, focused on the road, watery and far away, unsure. Normally, they're like windows to Ty's dark tortured soul, the one's that hot enough to scald, but that he never lets hurt me. And then there's his nose, straight and strong, solid, like his chin. That's not to say that Ty is overly masculine, but there's a straight edged cut to his features that makes him look tough, badass even.

I took all of this information in and held onto tight, desperate to keep as much of Ty's good side within me as I could because I had – *have* – a horrible feeling about what's to come. That sense is cemented when we climb out the doors and stand in the parking lot looking up at the tall, white building with the gray trim and the bright, red sign. It doesn't look cheerful, not in the least. See, I like old houses, Victorians and Craftsmen and whatnot because the way they were built makes them look like they're smiling. It's hard to explain, but the placement of the windows and the door and the accoutrement that accompanied houses in those days is just fucking cheerful as hell. This hospital, this bit of construction that can't rightfully be called *old* also can't be labeled as new. It sits somewhere between vintage and modern, this horrible piece of bad taste and a testament to the fact that not all architects are good designers.

Ty slips a cigarette into his mouth and does not offer me one, lights up with his purple lighter and sticks his blank hand into his pocket. His ringed beauty, which today is decorated with rhinestone speckled bracelets, sings in the clear air, clicking and ringing across the quiet parking lot which is dark with moisture and the threat of more rain. Very few people pull in nearby, very few enter that sad building, but those that do have gifts and smiles and woolen coats with fur trim.

Poor Ty, I think as I watch him, as I wish I'd gotten him

something impressive for Christmas, something that would take his world and turn it upside down like he did for me. Like a cat. I should've gotten him a cat then we really would've been the perfect family. Can't be complete without a cat. Instead, poor fucking Ty gets to visit his dying mother on Christmas, the one he hates, the one he blames for not being brave enough, for not seeing, for not caring.

Ty lifts his hand and grabs his cig with two fingers, lifts it away and closes his eyes as he exhales. Gray, gray smoke twirls in the air like a dancer, twists and turns, spins and rises to join the wet water clouds that hang above us threateningly. *In. Out. In. Out.* Ty takes his time and lets the gentle breeze ruffle his dark hair, kiss his cheeks, and move away, pulling a bit of his energy into the universe.

I don't rush him, and I don't speak. I stand very still and listen and watch; I push back my nausea and try to let this peaceful moment find a permanent home in my memory, a bit of something to look back on when I'm stressed. *The calm before the storm.* I adjust my black skirt, my green tee with the red Christmas tree and I used to wear half the year when I was in high school. I scoop my hair up into a ponytail and use a hair tie from my little, silver purse, the one that has no money but plenty of useless crap. I want to look good for Ty's mom, even if she is sick, even if he does hate her, I want to make sure that any memories of me with her son are good ones. *Of me and her grandkid.* I frown and touch a hand to my belly. When I look up, Ty is staring at me. He spins his lip ring around once and then sighs. It's not a sad sigh, though. Instead, he takes all of his pent up energy and pushes it out, lets the wind take that, too, and stands straight, broad shoulders back, chest out. Confident. My Ty looks confident.

"How about we go out to dinner after this?" he asks me as he easily closes the space between us, takes me in his arms, and tucks my head under his chin. "I think … I think I'll feel better then, you know? I just have to see her one more time, just one more fucking time, and I'm done with all of this shit. Then we can play merry fucking Christmas together and Skype your sisters up some wicked awesome New York cuisine."

"You have no idea how good that sounds," I tell Ty as I step back and take his hand. He leads the way across the parking lot with a peppier step, with determination that his past ends here and now and that, after he tells me everything, he'll be cleansed, fresh and ready to start anew. With me.

I can't wait.

17

Ty's mom is dead.

I'm sorry, says the stone faced doctor who doesn't really care. *But she went last night. We did everything we could.*

Ty now sits on a bench in the hallway with his face blank and empty, drained of that essential *Ty*-ness that makes him so fucking special. He sits there with his eyes wide and his shoulders hunched, his knees shaking just enough that I can see his nervousness but nobody else can.

"I – " I start to speak and Ty jumps like I've frightened him somehow. When he looks up at me, his gaze is unfocused and far away. "Why don't we get out of here?" I say, trying to smile. After all, most of Ty's pain has not come from his sadness. Melancholy like that is hard to cure, I know, but this disappointment, this fear, that he has can be erased if only he just lets it go. He didn't think he could move on until he saw his mother, but that just isn't true. He has the strength inside of him to move forward, and now, thanks to him, I have the strength inside of me to do the same. I don't sit down next to him or rub his back or anything like that. I can't nurture the state of mind that he's in. I have to do everything in my power to break him out of it. After all, life isn't always perfect. Sometimes it's bumpy and full of potholes, but if you drive carefully, you'll still make it to your destination. I have to impart this wisdom that I have somehow obtained.

I stare at Ty for awhile longer, missing him something fierce. Ever since he got that phone call, something has just been off … I miss him and he's right in front of me. Not good.

"Let's go to dinner and we can talk about it."

"I don't want to fucking talk about it," he says and pulls out a cigarette, ignoring the myriad *No Smoking* signs in his usual fashion. As soon as someone sees him, they're going to kick us the fuck out.

"Okay," I say as I watch him inhale. I can respect that. "Let's go find a restaurant crazy enough to be open on Christmas day and just let this all go." I pause. Here, now, it's time for me to speak up. "That important thing I wanted to tell you, I think it's time. Well, after we each have a glass of wine." I try to smile, but Ty keeps his frown.

"The only money I have for dinner is fuck money," he says which makes me step back. His voice is pitched at a normal tone, but there's something essential missing from his words.

It takes me a second to realize that it's heart. Ty is absolutely, one hundred percent *not* speaking from the heart; Ty *always* speaks from the heart. *Snap him out of this, Never. This is dangerous territory. You have both been there, done that. Get him out of it.*

"I don't care," I say, and this time, I really, really mean that. Ty's past is over and done with, end of sentence. There's a bit of silence where all I can hear is the buzzing of the florescent lights above our heads.

"Sure you don't," Ty says as he stands up and flicks his cigarette to the pristine, linoleum floor. I look at it and then at him, but he doesn't acknowledge his strange behavior or his harsh words. "Let's get the fuck out of here," he tosses over his shoulder as he moves away, leaving me standing there with a sick feeling in my belly. Maybe it's Ty's baby or maybe it's just me, I don't fucking know, but I don't follow after him. I might love him, and I might understand his pain, and fuck yes, he is my soul mate, but that does not give him an excuse to take his shit out on me.

Ty notices that I'm not following him when he gets to the end of the hallway and turns around, staring at me like he can't believe how hard I'm making this for him. I close my eyes slowly and think of the tractor, the way he changed Jade in a single afternoon; I think of Ty playing dress up with my little sisters and of the dog that he got me even though it was a stupid thing to do. *I fucking love this man, no matter what he says or does, and I just have to remember that.* I open my eyes again, letting happy memories play in them.

"Come pick up your cigarette," I tell him as I point down at the still burning cherry on the floor. It's Christmas day, so the staff at the hospital is minimal, and nobody has found us yet, but they will and I don't want them to see proof of Ty's disregard for their admittedly practical rule. There are plenty of reasons not to smoke in a hospital. Ty looks at me for a long, long while and then he turns on his heel and walks away.

Ty walks away from me, and I pick up his cigarette for him, put it out on the edge of a metal garbage can and toss it inside. Deep within me, old pain stirs and the stitches that Ty and my family have put in place begin to come loose. I touch my chip earring for comfort and pray to the souls of those that have come before me that I will make it out of this alive.

18

I have no idea where Ty is taking us, but he seems to know where he's going, and there is no way in fuck that I am going to ask. I was so pissed off at him that when I got outside, I dug through my purse until I found a cig, light it and smoked half of it before I realized that the only people I was hurting were my baby and me. I threw it to the cement and stomped on it, and climbed into the car where Ty was waiting, hands wrapped around the wheel. He smelled the cigarette smoke right away and gave me a very challenging glare that I ignored. Hell, he isn't even willing to admit that I'm pregnant, so what gives him the right to preach to me about it? He can talk about prenatal vitamins and ultrasounds when he actually acknowledges that I am carrying his child. Until then, well, until then, he can fuck off.

We turn off a four lane thruway that is understandably bereft of vehicles. After all, it's Christmas day and the sky is growing darker while the storm brews fiercer and the air holds a charge that convinces folks that it is in their best interest to stay indoors. Ty guides us down small side streets that grow greener by the block, filled with historic houses whose charm makes me smile as they slide past. Of course, then I hear Ty's bracelets jingle and I frown. I am royally pissed at him, but I am trying to be understanding. Remaining quiet seems like the best option right now. After awhile, I get tired of looking at houses and lay my forehead against the glass. Cooking Ty's offspring is a lot of work.

When I open my eyes again, the car is parked and the night sky is winking down at me, flashing stars sparkle like diamonds in the few spaces where the rainclouds have not taken over. Ty is nowhere to be seen, but there's a blanket on my lap, so I have hope of what I'll find when I climb out of the car. Ty has parked us at the top of a gravel driveway that comes off a garage that frames the yellow and white house that towers above me. It's awfully cold, so I wrap my arms around myself and take the blanket with me, unsure of where we are or why we're here. I already have the directions to our hotel programmed into the GPS on my phone. This place, wherever it is, is too quiet to be anywhere near NYC.

I move across the green grass, wet with dew, and shiver as the cold blades kiss my calves and make me wish I'd worn boots like Ty's. The front door is open, but the inside of the house is dark, making me a bit nervous as I approach the wrap around porch with the white columns.

"Ty?" I ask as I take the first step up and notice that while the house is beautiful from afar, up close it's a bit run down. The paint on the porch steps is chipped and peeling and the columns have definitely seen better days. If not mistaken, there's even one that looks like it might be leaning, if that's even possible. One of the big, beautiful windows in the front is cracked and covered with duct tape. Behind the glass hands a wrinkled sheet instead of curtains or blinds. From experience, I know that's a bad sign. Anyone who hangs sheets or blankets in their windows has questionable taste, especially when their front yard is as well manicured as this one. Somebody was hiding something here.

I hear breaking glass come from inside the house and pick up my pace, pausing as I hit the threshold and a horrible stench overwhelms me. It's a horrible potpourri of urine, garbage, and feces, and it forces me away and over to the pretty row of well trimmed hedges that hide the rotting wood of the porch railing.

I vomit over the edge and into the dirt, feeling guilty as I add to the horrible smell but unable to stop myself. I dump everything I have in me out and then dry heave and retch until my throat is sore and my belly feels like I've taken a beating.

"Shit," I curse as a wave of dizziness takes over me and makes me sway. Given the choice, I would be laying down right now, sleeping away this fatigue with Ty by my side and Angelica the pit at my feet. I turn around and lean back against the railing, closing my eyes and taking deep, long breaths until I can finally open my eyes without getting this horrible sense of vertigo sweeping down on me.

The sound of breaking glass has not stopped, so I force myself forward and into the house, pausing as I find out how difficult that simple action really is.

The house is packed from floor to ceiling with piles of *stuff* – garbage, boxes, books, clothing. You name it, this place has it. In *spades.* I cover my mouth with the edge of the blanket and start picking my way across the cluttered floor, cringing when I step on questionable lumps that squeak and crinkle and crunch. I don't call out for Ty, afraid to even speak in this veritable hell hole. I still don't know why we're here, but it doesn't take me long to figure it out. As I move by the impassable staircase, I see some framed pictures that were once probably quite nice but are now coated with a fine layer of dust and sticky cobwebs. When I reach out to touch one, I see that there's a familiar face among the grime.

Ty.

I rip one of the pictures from the wall, revealing a square of beautiful, cream wallpaper that probably once looked divine in this home. In Ty's grandma's home, the original owner of the rings that I now wear on my finger. I use my skirt to wipe away the grease and dirt and find a pair of dark brown eyes and a face that is cute but not *cutesy.* It was always pretty obvious that Ty was going to become a very handsome, young man. In this particular photo, my bad boy McCabe is free of butterflies and jewelery and instead clutches a pink elephant to his chest. He smiles, but he is not happy. That's obvious to me, even from this far away, even from this point in the future where the past Ty is as much a mystery to me as the location of the present.

More glass shatters and I know I can't wait any longer. Now that I know where I am and what this place is, I can make an educated guess about what's going on. I pause just long enough to pry Ty's picture from the frame and toss the dirty thing onto one of the nearby piles. I tuck the image into my shirt and forge onward, deeper into the dark, wondering why Ty hasn't turned on any lights. When I hit what I think was once the kitchen – based merely on my observation of dirty pots and pains, plates and cups, piles of dented cans, and a tower of white garbage bags that touches the ceiling and not on anything that you might expect like a stove or a fridge. I think there might be those things in here somewhere, but I will be damned if I can find them in this dark, dank disaster of a home. It's a shame really, a fucking pity. This house has history and charm and someone has just squatted and pissed all over it, taken expert craftsmanship and love and quality and destroyed it from the inside out. The people that lived here tried to poison Ty the same way they poisoned this home. Even in death, they are doing their best to ruin him.

I fight through the room and head towards the backdoor which sits ajar just enough that I catch a glimpse of moonlight from out back. That's where the sound of shattering hearts and glass is coming from. I press onward and squeeze myself out, nearly kill myself by stumbling down the steps and onto freshly mowed, green grass. The backyard is just as nice as the front, just as fake as the front, a facade for the neighbors and nothing more.

Ty stands in a small shaft of moonlight, like a spotlight, that peaks out of the clouds and highlights blue streaks in his ebony hair, shines along his cheekbones and turns his eyes to shadowy pits. He's throwing things at the fence – bottles, glasses, plates, picture frames. He has a small pile next to his feet, and he's picking them up one by one, pulling back his arm and letting them fly. His muscles flex and bulge with rage and pain and frustration as he lets loose his mother's clutter and watches it shatter into glittering sparkles that fall to the dirt below and disappear in the shadows of the fence.

I watch him for awhile before I say anything, measuring his mood and his ire until I think he's come down enough that he won't take too much of it out on me.

"Ty?"

He jumps and spins suddenly, blinking like he can't believe what he's seeing.

"Never?" he asks as if he hasn't seen me in years. Ty drops a white teacup to the grass and slumps to his knees. I go to him right away and pull his head against my belly, cradle him there and wait for him to speak.

"Tell me about it, Ty," I say, and when he tries to shake his head, I hold it still, lock him in place and make him face his fears. He has to if he wants to move on. The same way I confronted my father's murderer, Ty must face his fears and he has to conquer them with forgiveness and acceptance instead of anger and revenge. After all, anger and revenge are not healthy and even if I could condone them, Ty has no outlets. His demons are dead, and all that are left are their scars. "Tell me what happened to you."

19

Once upon a time, there was a boy who slept with a knife under his pillow and fear in his heart. He was twelve years old at the time, and he'd recently lost his cousin. He had a stepdad with unnatural thoughts and a mom who didn't love him as much as she should. This boy ... aw, fuck. This is no fucking fairytale. Let me give it to you straight. Might be hard though 'cause I feel so crooked right now, Nev, like I can't even think rational thoughts. There is all of this ... this crap inside my heart and I don't know how to process it. Can you help me? If I really, really ask for your help, if I lean on you, will I break you? That's the last thing I want, truly. I'm having terrible thoughts, Never. I keep thinking that I should go out and find another girl, throw my pain into her and let her deal with it after I leave. I feel like I shouldn't be burdening you with this stuff, but then ... I could never do that to you. Never, Never.

You want to know what happened to me, but I'm afraid you can't handle the gory details and the hands and mouths and cunts and cocks that made up my life and burned me up from within, used me up, and left me a broken shell of hurt and pain and shame. Never, you think you know me and maybe you do, maybe you know my soul and my heart and my pain, but you don't know the terrible things I was a part of. If I told you, would you still love? How could you? How could you love the boy whose stepfather came into his room and touched him there while he shook in fear and thought of his cousin and wished he was braver? How could you love the coward who cried while things happened to him that he didn't understand? Who took that knife and plunged it into the arm of that man and got him to stop just short of truly and utterly fucking him up?

That coward didn't finish what he started, didn't do the world a favor and take Satan's avatar out. Instead, he ran to his mother who didn't believe him, who punished him, who locked him in his room for days without food and water. And then he climbed out the window and disappeared into the arms of the street.

If he was looking for a loving presence, he was looking in all the wrong places. The boy learned some hard lessons there and did some unforgivable things. Will you still love him if you know? Will you?

20

I touch Ty's face, run my fingers through his hair and hold my eyes up to the sky, letting warm tears run down my face. When Ty talks about his mother and his stepfather and the things that happened to him, his voice changes and he becomes somebody else entirely. He morphs from this rock hard, street smart, tough guy to this softhearted boy who just wants to be loved. So, I haven't heard all of Ty's story, though I know I will, but I think I already know what's wrong with him. Tyson McCabe wants to be loved. It's that simple, but it's not that easy. Lucky him though because he's found me and I love him so much it makes me question whether any of this is even real. The hoarded house, I can deal with, the baby and school and money, I can deal with those too, but I cannot stand to have Ty so sad.

"Ty," I say, and my voice comes out so quiet and little. I tell myself that I'm not being selfish, that what I'm going to say next is all for him, but maybe it's for me, too. I cannot let the healing I've done be for naught. I grab hold of those stitches on my heart and press them down, staunch the bleeding with my own hand, something I have never, ever been able to do before. This time it's not just Ty, but me, too, and I'm proud of myself for it. "I'm pregnant."

Ty stops breathing for a moment. I know because his face is pressed into my belly and I can feel the warmth where his mouth is, right up against that spot where inside, something grows. Does he want it? Is he ready for it? Am I? Now that I've said what I need to say, maybe we can finally have a conversation about it. For the first time in my life, I feel like a grown-up.

"I know," he whispers finally, just as I'm about to step away and take a look at his face, try to judge the play of emotions there. Guys like Ty, these tortured hearts with bleeding souls who cannot make peace within themselves, are so easy to read. But then, Ty is changing, and he's becoming more complex. It's getting harder and harder to figure out what he's thinking. Maybe that's a good thing?

Ty stands up and wipes grass from the knees of his jeans. He doesn't look at me. Instead, he looks away and stares at the fence like all the answers are written there.

"I sort of figured that out when you stopped smoking … " he whispers and then, what I knew was coming. "Why didn't you tell me right away, Nev? I wanted you to so bad, babe. I

... I don't want you to think that I asked you to marry me just because of the baby, but I did want to make things easier for you. I wanted you to see that I was fucking here, that I ... "

"I'm sorry," I say, and I feel like a liar and a traitor with tears rolling down my face, fat and hot, and nausea roiling in my belly; my legs feel shaky and I collapse into Ty's arms where I try to fight, but where I can't because he's shushing me and hugging me so tight I feel like I might break.

"Goddamn it, Never Ross," he says, but his voice sounds better, more like Ty, more real. "You little bitch, don't you dare keep something like this from me ever again."

"Do you want me to get an abortion?" I ask him, sniffling and wishing that I wasn't relying on him so much. Surely, he'd like the chance to be vulnerable, too? But when I glance up and see him staring down at me with half-lidded eyes and a gentle smile, his dimples are deep and dark and happy. Ty wants to be strong for me.

"Fuck no," he says as he grabs my face and kisses me hot. "I want little Never babies with smart mouths and copper hair." I laugh and try to wipe my arm across my face, but he pushes it down and kisses me again, tasting, finding, keeping me. Ty moves his mouth slowly over mine, runs his tongue across my teeth and pulls back, so that he can stare at me again. This time, I think I see the shine of tears in his eyes, too, but the ass that he is, he doesn't let them fall.

"Guys don't cry, right?" I say and he wrinkles his nose at me, leaning forward and pressing his forehead into mine.

"Who fed you that crap?" he asks me, and I can't help but laugh. "We're the biggest babies on the planet. We just walk off and hide ourselves in bathrooms, bedrooms ... what do you think gentleman's club were for? Strippers, just therapists in disguise."

"I'm sorry," I tell him, but already, he's shaking his head

and his chest is swelling with a big ass breath.

"Don't be. I could've asked you about it. And to be fair, you tried, but I turned you down. I was so busy thinking about my mother ... " Ty swallows and can't speak for several moments, moments where we stand and just hold one another in silence. "Never, I wanted this," he touches my flat belly. "To be a special thing. I didn't want it tainted with all of this ... this *shit*." Ty flings his hand out at the house and shakes his head. "I just wanted to say goodbye to the bitch and forget her, but now ... now that she's gone, I think I'm finally realizing that I wanted her to see me, too. Before she went, I wanted her to see that I was okay, that I'd survived, so that she'd be okay, too. I hated my mom, Never, but I know that deep down, there was a good person buried under all that insecurity and desperation. Wherever she is now, I hope she knows that I know that. I can see it in those photographs."

I touch Ty's rings, run my thumb across the metal and take them in. I hope he never stops wearing them. They've become more than just jewelry. Those rings are a piece of Tyson Monroe McCabe and I'm a greedy bitch; I want all of him that I can get.

"You can't hold onto her," I tell him though I feel harsh saying it granted that she only just passed away. Ty needs a heavy hand though. He isn't a guy that wants to be tiptoed around or lied to. "You have to cut her off and let her go. You can still love her and care about her and think about her, but you can't let her rule your life."

"I know, right?" he whispers as he pulls me against him again and hugs the bejesus out of me. "Now I have to think about diapers and shit." I laugh, but I know that we've only just touched on that situation. Ty says he wants copper haired babies, but does he really?

"What about school?" I ask him, unable to believe that my

problems can be solved so quickly. I expected Ty to blow up, to walk out of this yard, drive away and fuck some hussy bitch. Why? Because that's what I would've done had our positions been reversed. Hell, that's why Ty would've done if he was the Ty from a few months ago. But he's not. And neither am I. We're changing and growing together, intertwining our branches so that from far away, it looks like we're one in the same. "We can't live in the dorms with a baby." Ty pauses and looks over at the house.

"Nope," he says. "But then, I got us a damn pit anyhow, so I guess we need a house ... " Ty keeps his gaze on the yellow siding, the white trim, the shadowed windows. "Which is good because ... " He trails off and raises his hand, indicating the building with a jingle of his bracelets. "This piece of shit, this is mine." Ty turns to me with an expression that is halfway between a grimace and a smile. "We might have to clean it up a bit." He pauses. "Well a lot, but I'm used to that." I look at Ty and then at the house, and I think about the story he told me about cleaning his apartment.

"School?" I ask because I have to be the practical one if Ty is going to be the dreamer, if he's going to tell me that everything is okay just as I want him to. He grins nice and big and sweeps me up in his arms, spins me around and keeps me there with my feet lifted off the ground just so, just enough that it feels like I'm weightless.

"This is a college town, babe. We can transfer, can't we?"

"Maybe ... " I begin.

"No," Ty says, and his voice is firm. "No, not maybe. If we decide to this, we're going to do it, and babe, I know we can do it. With you around, man, I could do fucking anything." And that is all the talking that Ty McCabe wants to do tonight. He kisses me again, pushing his tongue into my mouth and taking charge, squeezing me tight so that my hips are pressed against him and my back is arched. Even if I had the strength to fight him, to talk about the unpleasant tasks that no doubt lie before us, I just can't. Right now, I want to live in this fairytale. I want to fuck Ty in the backyard of this less than ideal house that was his grandma's, that, just like his rings, Ty will take and make beautiful. I hardly have any idea what town I'm in and yet, I'm sold. I'm sold because Ty is here. Home is where the fucking heart is, right? And in Ty's chest, I know mine beats a symphony of love that's pitched just right, so that only I can hear. My Ty. Mine.

I kiss him back and wrap my arms around his neck, kiss him like the fairytale prince that every girl wants. His horse might be black instead of white and he isn't blonde haired and blue eyed, but damn it, he has butterflies inked into his skin and birds on his back, an eyebrow and a lip ring, and words of wisdom peppered with the foulest fucking language known to man. I would take Ty McCabe over a knight in shining armor any day.

"Guess I can skip the condoms for awhile?" he whispers as I let him pull away for a split second, just one split second so that he can lay me on my back in grass of the backyard next to his discarded teacup. The house might be trashed but out here, it feels like we're the only two people in the world. I don't hear any traffic or barking dogs, children or late evening joggers. It's blissfully peaceful, and the night is shared simply with the moon and the clouds which promptly begin to rain on the two of us.

Ty raises his eyebrow, the one with the ring, and without words, connects with my eyes and knows that I don't give a shit, that if he stops, he'll have a lot worse to worry about than a bit of rain.

We kiss again and Ty tangles his fingers with mine, raises them over my head and presses them into the dewy grass which soaks into my shirt and skirt, teases my bare legs and neck. He holds me down with his warmth and I hardly notice the icy rain that splatters against my cheeks, against Ty's sable hair, his strong back. I am hot from the inside out, and I think I've even begun to sweat. Ty does that to me, makes me so hot I can barely stand it, like I'm standing too close to the sun.

We have a lot to talk about, to figure out, but don't most couples? Wouldn't it be boring if there was nothing at all for us to discuss? Ty and I are engaged, *engaged,* so that makes us partners. This, this baby thing should be crushing me, scaring the shit out of me, snapping me back to reality, but I can't seem to shake this blessed feeling I have because Ty is by my side.

Our mouths are communicating in a different way now, playing off one another with tongue and lips and teeth, exploring. We exchange breath and in doing so, we share a part of ourselves. Chills run up and down my arms, tease the fine hairs on the back of my neck and draw my legs apart, so I can welcome Ty into me, take him to a different place, heal him with the very thing that used to bleed him. Strange that something we both used as a weapon before has now become a balm during the best of times and a leisure activity at the worst. Pretty incredible. I wonder what Vanessa, our Sexual Obsession Group leader, would think if she knew how far we'd come. And to be honest with you, that's the last logical thought I have as Ty releases me and moves his wet hands under my soggy shirt, explores my flesh with his fingertips, reading me with his body as he explores and savors the moment in all its strange, fucking glory.

We're making out. Us. The two biggest whores in California. We're just kissing because it feels so damn good to be able to do just that, and when my hands get restless, I follow Ty's suit and slip them under his shirt and along the hard muscles of his taut belly, the one that stays so perfect even though he never works out. I know, though, that even if he were to lose those muscles, that lip ring, those tattoos, that I would still love him. I was attracted to Ty because he was beautiful but damaged, pretty but broken, but I fell hard for him because he is the most tortured, bloody, fucking amazing individual I have ever met. Hard to top that.

I moan into Ty's mouth as he finally kicks up our session a notch and frees my breast from the confines of my bra, massaging it in circles, digging the metal of his rings into the soft flesh. I sigh against him, relaxing my body and dropping my hands, sensing Ty's need to be in control. I have no problem surrendering to him. That's what love is really. Surrendering yourself to the person that means the most to you. Appropriate or not, a piece of Noah's poetry sounds in my head, the perfect lyrics to the song Ty and I are singing with our bodies. It's another line from *For Them The Wheel Turned*, the very same poem I was quoting to myself when Ty first took me to SOG. Talk about coming full circle.

And the unwashed found refuge in capitulation; and they were ecstatic in their state because it made them bigger than the self; connecting them to their other halves, this process built hearts and souls and became their reason for living.

A sigh of pleasure escapes my lips, built on poetry and passion, lifted from my body by Ty's fingers as he drags them down my stomach. I'm certain that he's going for the zipper of his pants because, well, that's what Ty and I always do. Instead, he lifts up his shirt and lets it flop into the grass in a heavy, wet pile, leaving his upper body slick and moist, lit up with silver starlight and the kiss of the moon.

I sit up, too, just enough that I can run my hands along Ty's shoulders, feel the twitch of hard muscle beneath smooth skin that I know he must shave but never lets me catch him doing it. I touch that lone bit of hair below his bellybutton, slide my arms around his waist and press my ear to his chest, so that I can hear his heart beating. He leaves me there for a moment and then he's wrapping my hair around his wrist and pulling me back to look at me.

"Your red and black hair turned my head, Nev," he tells me as he examines my face with half lidded eyes and turns up the corner of his mouth. "But your carpet don't match your drapes, so ... "

I snort and slap him lightly, grabbing his chin fiercely in my fingers.

"Are you saying you want me to stop dying my hair or that you want me to put a nice, bright streak in my pubes?"

"I'm just saying that it might be awkward when your ob-gyn gets down there and calls you on it." Ty grins and opens his mouth again. I kiss him hard, knocking our teeth together, determined to keep him from ruining the moment with admittedly funny but terribly crude humor. If I have to push out his love child, the least he can do is show me a good time.

"Shut up and fuck me," I whisper with his lower lip tucked between my teeth, lip ring clinking against the enamel. "Now."

Ty rips off my shirt like an animal in heat, puts his hand on my chest and pushes me back into the wet grass that is quickly becoming mud as the downpour intensifies and sticks our hair to our foreheads and slicks Ty's jeans against his ass.

"I think we need to practice foreplay," he whispers, droplets of moisture clinging to his skin, hugging him tight and slipping down his skin. "I don't want you going behind my back and telling all your fucking sisters that I am a *wham, bam, thank you, ma'am* sort of a guy. Beth already looks at me funny."

"She looks at you funny because you curse like a sailor and

try to sneak smokes in the downstairs bathroom."

"There's that, too," Ty says as he retrieves a cigarette from his back pocket along with a lighter. He wiggles the objects at me with a grin. "Going to give you a vicarious postcoital smoke."

"Postcoital?" I ask him, trying to use my elbows to prop up, so I can raise an eyebrow and give him my signature bitch look. I'm starting to get mad horny, and I'm going to blame him for making me pregnant. "You haven't even fucked me yet." Ty ignores me, manages somehow to light up in the pouring fucking rain because he's just so friggin' amazing at everything, and then pushes me back into the grass.

"Oh, I'll get there, baby, but it's a process." I try to remind myself that his mother died today, and he needs to be in control of something, so hell, it might as well be me right now. I relax my muscles, and then gasp as Ty slides two fingers in me, just like that. He pushes aside my underwear and makes himself at home, slipping all the way into his knuckles and hitting my pulsing flesh with his hand as he moves in and out. He starts off wicked fast and then slows, hooking his fingers, so that he's teasing the muscles that clench and squeeze just for him, tightening and releasing, begging him to release whatever it is that he might have inside of me. With his other hand, Ty smokes. He fucking smokes and teases me in more ways than one. Even through the wall of water that cascades from the sky and cuts the clouds up into shards, I can smell tobacco and bad boys, pasts that burn like lava, and the scent of my own desire.

I let him bring me to the edge of my sanity, to the spot where I once thought I would jump from, crash to the rocky floor of my own mind and let myself die there. This time, when my feet slip and my body becomes weightless, I soar.

21

"The only reason that you're not dead is because of that kiss," I tell Ty as he rolls off of me and collapses into the mound of white pillows at our backs. I turn towards him, drawing my knees up towards my chest and sliding my hands under my head. I am just this side of sore down there, gently bruised by Ty's thrusts, the pressure of his hips, the strength of his love for me. Each time I adjust myself a get a reminder that he was inside of me and have to smile. "The one that you gave me after you put my shirt back on. I think you actually said *mwah*. I didn't know anybody actually made sound effects for their own kisses."

"See," Ty says, chest rising and falling as he tries to recover from the vigorous exercise that he's just undergone. "Disney fucking prince. I told you I was lame." I reach over and poke at his lip ring, but I do it with affection. After all, Ty just taught me a new position, one that he swears comes from the Kama Sutra, but that I think he really just made up. He smiles, like he senses my thoughts, and turns over, a cigarette magically appearing in his hands. Pretty impressive, considering the fact that he's naked. "Thank your boyfriend for this hotel," Ty says as he puts the cig in his mouth and kisses me with it dangling from his lips. He's teasing me on purpose, the ass. "This shit is posh." I don't look around the room to confirm his statement. Despite the fact that we were shirtless and rearing to go when we stumbled in, we both still managed to get quite the shock when we saw the room. Posh was right. Noah had spared no expense.

"Fuck you," I say softly, but he knows I don't mean it. "Your thick skull just isn't used to down pillows. It's making you testy."

"Riiight," Ty says, snapping his teeth together and rolling over to dig through his discarded jeans in search of a lighter. When he returns, the glow of the cigarette illuminates his face in the darkness. He takes a breath, like he's about to say something and then just stops. Silence descends. I fill it first because I know that now is the time to get some of the serious crap out and on the table. We won't be able to do it all at once; Ty and I are not built like that. It will have to come in stages, like Ty's past. Yet another thing we need to discuss.

"I'm sorry that I lied to you," I tell him and tears come, hot and fresh. I'm glad he can't see them in the dim light. Today is not about me. This is about Ty, and I've already taken up too much of the spotlight. His mother died yesterday and left him with an inheritance of guilt and pain and a hoarded house that used to belong to his beloved grandmother. He has a right to be feeling it, yet now, he's acting like it's no big deal. Do I think he's hiding some of his emotions? Hell yes. Is he ready to go off the deep end? Maybe not. Ty is stronger than me. Where it took me weeks to recover, I can only guess that he will be okay in a few days.

"It was an omission of truth," he says, trying to make me feel better. "And besides, I was the fuckwad that stopped you in your moment of courage." He pauses. "And I'm sorry, too." Ty turns over and finally sees the tears on my face. With a deep, throaty chuckle he reaches out and brushes his fingertips along my wet cheeks. "Are you okay, baby?" he asks me, voice too soft to be real. It's at odds with his dark hair and eyes, his tattoos, his piercings. He should be thanking me and getting up, grabbing his clothes and leaving. That's what they've always done to me. Men. But not Ty. Somehow, in that bar way back when, I found one of a handful of real people, the ones from legend who care about others and put their needs before their own. How lucky am I?

I decide to tell Ty the truth, even if it hurts him because I cannot lie again. Or omit the truth. Whatever.

"I don't want to be pregnant," I say and my stomach flip-flops as if in protest. "I'm afraid. I don't know how to be a mom, Ty. You don't know how to be a dad. We have no money. We – " Ty shushes me with a kiss, putting his hands on either side of my face. Cigarette ash hits the perfect pillows beneath us.

"Never, being a mom means putting someone else's needs before your own. You can do that, I know you can. You've done it for me." Already, I'm shaking my head.

"When?" I ask as I delve into the depths of Ty's dark eyes and look for truth in his statement. I feel like I've been a selfish bitch from day one.

"By coming here with me for one," Ty tells me. "For leaving your sisters and coming halfway across the country to a big, steaming pile of shit."

"But ... " I try to say something, but I'm not sure what words need to cross my lips. I had to be here with Ty. I just had to. There was no real debate, no animosity, just this simple need to stand by his side. Is that what it's like to be a mother? Is it much the same as being a sister? Love is love, after all. The results of it may have different manifestations and different outcomes, but isn't it all the same?

"To be a good parent," Ty says, and I wonder where he's getting this from because he seems pretty damn sure of himself. "You have to believe in your kids. You have to trust them and they have to trust you, and the rest of the world be damned, you have to stand up for them no matter. If they fuck up, you have to hold their hand and show them that it's okay, show them how to do it right. And the last bit, the most important one is real easy. Nev, when I said you had the greatest capacity to love of any human being I have ever met, I meant that shit. You and your sisters are a site for sore friggin' eyes, a dot of color in a world of black and gray. You already have the perfect ingredients inside of you to be a good mother. I see it in your face when you hold Darla, when you laugh with Jade, when you kiss me. You have to fucking love them, Nev. That's all there really is to it."

Ty rolls back over and flicks his cigarette onto the nightstand. There are no ashtrays in a room as fine as this.

"How do you know?" I ask him because what he says sounds easy and yet, my mother couldn't do it. His mother couldn't do it. There has to be something else, something that makes it hard. Besides, how can Ty possibly know? How, how, how?

"Because when you've been with someone as selfish and ignorant as my mother, it's easy to find her complete opposite in a crowd." My own words flash through my mind, a silent reminder of one of the simple truths I've always known. *If you live your whole life in the darkness, then you don't have any trouble recognizing the light.* I scoot forward a bit, so that I can lay my head on Ty's chest and revel in the idea that I have the other half of my soul lying right next to me, telling me that things are going to be okay, loving me back with every fiber of his being. "What else?" he asks, and his muscles contract as he leans over the bed and gets another cigarette. My mouth waters, but I'm craving the secondhand smoke, so I let him have it. "I can feel your stress," he tells me. "Let it all out."

"This is about you," I say, determined to get him to talk about his feelings. He's having them, even if he won't admit it.

"Fuck that," Ty says as his bracelets clink and he blows out a puff of smoke that hangs in the stagnant air like a cloud. "I'm your right hand right now, your support beam. Nev, you have my baby on board." Ty turns on his side again, dislodging my head but putting his nose so close to mine that I can't complain because I can see his face clear as day, and he looks pretty happy about what he's just said. Proud maybe, too.

"Think you're some kind of stud or something?" I ask and forget all about practical shit until I really just want to flick him in the balls and see how high pitched he can scream. Ty raises both eyebrows at me and props his head up on a hand. His look is all male arrogance and sex – half sexy and half annoying as fuck.

"You said you fucked more than forty guys?"

"Don't want to talk about this right now."

"And didn't use protection, right?"

"I was on the pill."

"And on our what, our second fuck, you got pregnant?"

"You're an ass." Ty laughs and the sound is joyous enough that I have to fight back a smile.

"I got you pregnant," he says, like he just can't say it enough.

"Stop."

"I marked you. You're mine. I like that. I like knowing that my baby is growing inside of you, that a piece of me will always be tied with a piece of you."

"If that's true then you owe me," I say getting brief but terrifying glimpses of me, legs spread, on a table surrounded by doctors with a freaking *person* screaming from between my thighs. I feel sick. "God," I groan as I push away from Ty and stumble to the bathroom. As usual, he's right behind me, right there by my side, strong and immovable, a force to be fucking reckoned with.

"I agree," he says as he brushes hair from my forehead. "And I concede. Whatever it is that you want, I'll give it to you."

"I want you," I gasp, sucking in mouthful after mouthful of breath as I fight back nausea. I have the weirdest urge, bent over that toilet like an invalid. Either I just have odd taste buds or the cravings have already started. "To get me a fucking strawberry shake."

22

The next morning when I wake up, I am no longer sweetly sore but painfully sore, and I have to slap Ty hard on the arm to feel better about it. At least, to his credit, the man has breakfast waiting for me on the table that overlooks the city, perched high on a balcony I would never venture onto if it weren't for Ty. That's not to say that I'm afraid of heights but rather that before all of this happened, all of this stuff with Tyson McCabe, I craved them. I had always wanted to see what it would feel like to throw myself off, to be weightless for just a single moment in time. That's not to say that I was suicidal – or maybe I was and just didn't know it – but really, I wanted to see what it would be like to take the weight off my shoulders for awhile. With Ty here, I feel like he's sharing the burden with me and that, while the load of life's problems and insecurities will never be fully lifted, now it's not such a big deal because he's standing beside me.

"Thanks for the shake," I say, grabbing my second dose of strawberry. The first I didn't even get to finish because Ty shoved me up against a wall, pressed my cheek to the gold and brown wallpaper and fucked the shit out of me. It was the second best fuck of my life, topped only by the first time we made love. I don't think that one will ever lose it's number one spot, though I sure would like to see Ty try.

"Thanks for the bake," he says and when I stare at him with a raised eyebrow, he rushes to explain. "You know, shake and bake?" I keep staring. "Okay, not fucking funny," he says as he blows air out from between his teeth. He's dressed to kill today, so it really doesn't matter how lame his jokes are. He's got on this long sleeved shirt which shouldn't be sexy because it covers the muscles in his arms but somehow is anyway because he wears bracelets over the top of it, and the butterflies peek out at me from the end of the sleeve, tantalizingly reclusive. Besides, the fabric is tight and clings to him, outlining his pecs and his belly muscles. He's paired it with baggy jeans that are holier-than-thou, tucked into his big, black combat boots.

I sit in his lap because frankly, there is nowhere else I'd rather be, and lean my head against his. He doesn't know it, but last night, I heard him get up and stand on this balcony. He didn't cry, but he mourned. I could feel his melancholy energy like a storm, so I cried for him. Maybe I'm just hormonal, but to me, it seemed as if his pain was my pain. My poor Ty.

I sip the shake and notice that there's a map on the table, marked up with red lines and little dots.

"S'that?" I mumbled around my red straw. Ty cringes which is weird enough and stuffs a miniature muffin into his mouth. Continental breakfast anyone? They have the weirdest shit.

"It's our tour for the day," Ty tells me and his voice is falsely cheerful like he wants to be happy but can't. I wonder what happened between now and last night.

"Tour?"

"The time line of my past," he says and then pauses. "Or part of it anyway. There's some baggage back in California, but I figure if we start with this then you'll know and then I can just forget it all and move on."

"I don't understand."

"Never, I was a whore. A fucking whore. A prostitute. I fucked people for money. I did it because I didn't know what else to do. I let weakness and pain overwhelm me. I need you to see where I'm from."

"Just tell me about it," I say. I don't want to visit the places that Ty frequented, run into people he might have slept with. The thought makes me sick to my stomach. Or maybe that's just Ty or Never Junior down there. "I don't want to see."

"Maybe not," he tells me. "But I need you to." I try to change the subject.

"What about your mother's house?" I ask. Ty pretty much flat-out said we could live there, go to school, raise our kid. It sounds good in theory, but in practice, the place is a festering shit hole of crap. Worse than the actual garbage are the memories that Ty is going to have dredged up by the whole process. What if we find things in there? Things that he doesn't want to see? That he isn't ready to see?

"We'll clean it out, together," he tells me, voice strong and confident, like he's made up his mind and there is no going back. It's a false sense of security that could crumble at any moment. I need to be the mortar that holds it all together. "And if it's liveable," he says and then chokes on the word. That house has a lot of bad memories in it. I wonder if that's such a wise idea. "We move in. If not, we sell the property as is, retreat back to Cali and make a go of it."

"Can you live there?" I ask him. "Can you honestly tell me that the ghosts of your past won't haunt you?"

"They might," he says, but I can tell he's already thought about it. "But I'm willing to bet my sanity on the fact that you and me, we could handle it. It's a *house,* Never. If my mom hasn't fully fucked it, then it's a historical freaking landmark, an heirloom that my grandmother left us, so that we'd have a fighting chance in this world. It'll be ours, just ours, free and fucking clear. We can go to school and raise our kid without having rent as a fucking overhead." He pauses here for dramatic effect. "And I can even buy you *Baby Einstein* episodes or some shit." I laugh, but he isn't done. Ty stands up, taking me with him and leans me up against the railing, not on it per se because I can feel that he isn't willing to risk me thirty stories up. He lets me feel the wind in my hair and his warm breath on my neck. "Or maybe some sexy lingerie to wear when you're big and pregnant?" I slap him lightly. "No? How about some classical music to make sure the brat's smart?"

"Ty," I say, but I laugh because I can't help it. Ty makes me want to laugh. "You're an asshole," I tell him and he nods like this is common knowledge.

"That's true," he says. "But I'm an asshole that's engaged to you, bound and determined to stick by your side forever.

You are pretty much stuck with me whether you like it or not, babe."

"I like it," I reassure him.

"Then come with me and let me show you my dark side."

"I've already seen it," I whisper, my voice suddenly hoarse.

"No," he tells me. "You haven't. And I need you to." Here he pauses and plays his sympathy card. I pretend that it's the only one he's got, but in reality, he has as many as he needs. "Please, Nev. I can't confront my mom, and I sure as fuck can't confront that douche bag of a husband she dragged out of the gutter, not until I get to hell anyway, but I can confront the streets and the life that nearly killed me. Tell me you'll come with. If you don't, I'm afraid I'll get stuck again." Even though Ty's already got my heartstrings wrapped around his fingers, he tugs on them with his eyes, giving me this look that is so fucking puppy dogs and kitty cats sappy that I have no choice but to relent.

"Okay," I say. "But in exchange, I want a tattoo."

"No." Ty says that single word with such force that we both cringe. And then I get pissy because I'm not going to play pregnant bitch to his masculine stud.

"You gonna stop me?" I ask as I push away from him and drop to the cement floor beneath our feet. Ty looks at me defiantly.

"Remember how I said I wasn't into tying chicks up?"

"You're a weirdo," I begin, but he isn't done.

"I am now. If you try to get a tat, I will tie you up and pleasure you fiercely for days. Tattoos are bad news for babies, Nev. How about after it's born? I'll save some fuck money for you." I don't tell Ty that his threat is actually kind of tempting. Instead, I cross my arms defiantly and glare. After all, I am Never Ross and that's what I do. I am an ornery bitch with a dirty past and a whole shit ton of rage just waiting to break loose.

"Not good enough," I say as I cross my arms over my chest and hear the distinct ringing of my phone from inside the hotel room. "A piercing?" Ty shakes his head.

"Even worse."

"What then?" I ask him and he grins.

"Remember what you said about marking me … ?"

23

A few hours later, Ty walks out of the tattoo parlor with *Never say Never* tattooed across the back of his neck. He says it didn't hurt, but I don't believe him. I'm getting good at reading McCabe's body language, identifying the slight muscle twitches in his face, the curl of his ringed fingers, the pacing of his breath. It hurt like a bitch, but he did it for me.

"I would've put *Property of Never Regali-Ross-McCabe* or whatever the hell else you might've wanted. It didn't have to be so subtle," he tells me, but already, I'm shaking my head. I didn't have him get a more specific tattoo not because I was afraid we might break up one day or because I was afraid it was too personal or anything that stupid and shallow. I had him get that tattoo because it's like an inside joke between us, something that others will see but few will understand. For Ty and myself, there is no breaking up or separating. We are not just engaged; we are entangled. And now we're starting to develop our own language, a language spoken in cryptic phrases and subtle shoulder rolls. Like any good couple, we're developing. This tattoo is just a part of a larger picture.

"I know," I tell him. "And that's one of the reasons that I love you so much." Ty sighs and puts a hand over his heart, batting his long, dark eyelashes at me.

"Say it again," he tells me as we pass through crowds of people who are so similar in their actions that it's eerie, almost as if they're extras in a movie, following the director's shouted orders. They have two choices: stare straight ahead with eyes wide and faces tense, pretend they're not interested in anything when what's really happening is that they're dying for *something,* and the others, well, they walk with their faces buried in their devices, glowing screens highlighting their tired, overworked faces. *Welcome to New York.*

"I love you," I say simply and am pleased at the reaction on Ty's face, the warm, fuzzy look that makes him shiver and press my knuckles to his lips. My bracelets, the ones that Ty gave me this morning, ring like bells. They're silver with purple stripes and they match my shirt so perfectly that I'm sure that Ty's had this planned for awhile. We match, just enough that we look like we belong together; not so much that we look related. It's a nice place to be. "I want a butterfly tattoo," I admit to him as we walk down the street, hand in hand, towards the place where Ty says the story of his life as a street worker really begins. "Something big, something bright." I pause and see that Ty's smile is slipping and not because of me. He's trying to look at me, to pay attention, but in the last few seconds, something else has caught his eye. It takes me awhile to figure out what it is, but as we cross the street, I finally realize. It's an apartment building.

It towers above us, a cheerless rectangle of red-brown stucco and glass with balconies galore, most of them filled to the brim with potted plants, BBQs and bistro tables. There's nothing special about it, at least not to me. It's a fairly new building, not too high end but certainly not anything you might call questionable. People come and go in droves, leading children by the hands and dogs by leashes as they move from cabs to revolving glass doors and back again.

"Here," Ty tells me as he stops next to a coffee shop that sits smashed between a small boutique and a shoe store. It looks small but cozy, intimate, like the coffee they sell just has to be good because the place is so damn cute. "I want to stop here and tell you my story."

24

I was such a naïve, little fuck. I really, truly believed that my mother would dump the douche and come looking for me, take me into her arms and tell me she was sorry for everything. Sorry that she'd killed my one and only friend in the world, that she'd been distracted with devils but was now singing choir with fucking angels.

What a load of shit.

I survived for awhile by dumpster diving and hanging out at the library. Sometimes I went to school; mostly I didn't.

Then I met Hannah.

Let me tell you about Hannah first because you're going to judge her which is fine because to be honest, she has problems, lots of them. She likes young boys. Not like little kid young, but too young, thirteen, fourteen. When I met her I told her I was fifteen; she knew I was lying.

Hannah felt sorry for me because I was dirty and unwashed, my clothes stank, and I was getting skinny as hell. I was not the type of twelve-just-turned-thirteen year old that they write adventure books about, that survive in the wilderness with nothing but a fuckin' hatchet. I had no life skills of which to speak, and a terrible desperation to be rescued. That's why I fell for Hannah.

The first time she met me, she bought me food and clothes and gave me her phone number. The second time she met me, she took me up to her apartment and let me stay the night on her couch. I snuck out before she woke up and remembered I was there. The third time I met Hannah, she gave me a hundred dollars to go into her bedroom and have sex with her. I had my first time right up there on the twenty-second floor with a woman ten years my senior with psychological problems galore and a very deep connection with the local sex scene.

I spent fifty of that hundred bucks at the arcade and used the rest to buy shitty fuck food from the store. It had been fun, Hannah was chill, and needless to say, I was hooked.

25

Ty sips his black coffee, savoring the taste in his mouth, eyes closed, lips pursed. I ignore mine and peel my eyes away from him, so that I'm staring into the steaming mug and not at the memories on his face. If Ty were a mirror, I would be seeing my own reflection of shame and mistakes and missteps. He is just like me, and I think that's why this hurts so much. I know *exactly* what he's going through, what he went through, and how those memories can sometimes feel like a noose around your neck.

"Whatever happened to Hannah?" I ask as Ty's dark eyes are revealed ever so slowly as his lids draw apart and his face goes white-as-fuck. He even drops his cup and hot, scalding coffee goes everywhere. He stands and curses, but he doesn't take his eyes off of the space behind my head. When I turn, I feel as if I'm moving in slow motion, stuck in the time warp that is Ty's memory and frozen there with shackles of pain on my wrists and ankles.

There is a woman standing in the doorway with pretty, honey colored curls that frame her pale face. She has long, thin lips that would look out of place on most people but which fit her pointy chin and dangerously sharp cheekbones. She's older than Ty and me, but she isn't *old,* not really. I'm guessing that she's in her early thirties. That she lives on the twenty-second floor of the apartment building that Ty could not stop staring at. That her name is Hannah.

She recognizes him right away, I can tell. Her pastel green eyes find his dark ones and get stuck there the same way that his are stuck on hers. My baby goes crazy, pushing bile into my throat and making me feel like I'm going to pass out from dizziness. He's only a month old and the little fuck is trying to tear me down. I stand up suddenly and stumble. Ty is there, of course. Not even the sight of his first trick can make him forget me. I know that and yet, I want to fucking kill Hannah. I want to murder her in the middle of the quaint little coffee shop on the West-East-Whatever Side of Who-the-Fuck-Cares New York district. I want to pick up the knife that the lady sitting nearest to me is using to butter her croissant, and I want to stab Hannah between the eyes.

Is it jealousy? Maybe. Is it disgust? Oh fuck yeah, it's that, too.

You corrupted him, I think, knowing there are worse ways

to be corrupted. *You pushed him down a hill that it's taken years to climb back up. He doesn't love you, and he never will. When he moved inside you, it was without thought, a simple, primal function that he could not understand because he wasn't old enough, you cow.*

"Hannah," Ty says as he lifts me up and tucks me under his chin, soaking my shirt and skirt with coffee. One of the baristas is handing Ty a wet cloth with one hand and mopping up his mess with the other. I feel sorry for her.

"Tyson," she says, giving me the distinct impression that Ty took on his nickname later in life. I can see why he dislikes being called Tyson. It reminds him of *this*. "Funny seeing you here," she says nonchalantly, like she didn't devirginize a freaking *child*. I want Ty to scream at her, to beat her up, to call her out on her dirty deeds. Instead, he smiles. It's dimple free, but it's still a smile. "I heard you'd moved to California?"

"I did," he says simply, and since he isn't paying any attention to the barista, I'm the one that has to take the wet cloth and clean us up. "But I'm thinking of moving back." I press the cloth pretty forcefully against his chest. In a city this large, we just happened to stumble upon this bitch? I find that pretty hard to believe. *Say something, Never.*

I spin around and manage to grab Hannah's eyes. In her, I see pain reflected back at me. She is the way she is because something – or more likely *someone* – made her that way. The thought makes me sick, but I can't feel sympathetic towards someone that would fuck a thirteen year old homeless kid. It just isn't happening. I hold Hannah's eyes with a fiery gaze, lock her into my orbit until she starts to fidget and look around the room, trying to find something other than me to focus on. She stares at the oversized, burgundy velvet armchairs in the corner next to planter boxes filled with bamboo. She marvels at the floor to ceiling shelves of coffee in bags and cans and cups. She enjoys the local artwork on the wall, the framed bits of paper that look like scribbles but have four digit price tags. Hannah looks at anything but Ty and me.

"I guess we better be going," Ty says from behind me, and as soon as I hear his voice, I snap out of my death glare and turn to him, wanting to throw myself in his arms and claim him. The only thing that keeps me calm is the tattoo. Knowing that he's marked permanently with ink makes me feel better. Still, my behavior is a bit alarming, and I'm forced to blame it on the pregnancy to avoid guilt. I have a feeling I'll be doing that a lot for the next few months. Could be my lack of nicotine though. Actually, there's a very, very good chance that it may be that.

Hannah steps out of the way, a vision in her chiffon sun dress that is so inappropriate for the weather I can't even begin to tell you, and reaches into her purse.

Ty moves us forward, eyes still locked on his first client in a way that disturbs the shit out of me, and as we pass, Hannah reaches out and takes his hand. I nearly slit her throat right then and there.

"Hands off," I snap as she scribbles some lines on the back of Ty's beautiful, butterfly hand. When she sees the tattoos, she smiles, and I'm forced to shove her back and draw the attention of the entire coffee shop. Silence descends.

"My number," she says as I resist the urge for violence and push my way out the door and onto the street with Ty stumbling behind me. As soon as we hit pavement, I slap him. Hard.

"Wipe it off," I snap.

"Never," he begins as he tries to reach out for me. I move away.

"Wipe it of."

"I didn't expect to see her here, honestly. It was a one in a million chance. I just wanted to show you where it happened."

I step forward, get into Ty's personal space and steal a cigarette. When he tries to stop me, I move back and grab a lighter out of my purse.

"Never, don't," Ty pleads, and his voice is so soft and broken that I know I should comfort him. This is hard for me; it must be agony to him. Unless he wants to talk to Hannah, to see her. Maybe he has Stockholm syndrome or some shit? I turn away and light up. "Please." That one word stops me in my tracks and turns my head around. Ty doesn't wipe off the number whether because he's frozen, stuck in rotten memories and beleaguering agony, or because he doesn't want to, I don't know. I drop the cigarette where it joins a whole host of others on the ground. I feel bad for doing it, but right now, I just don't care.

"I want to kill her," I tell him honestly. Nobody stops and stares or even seems to hear my violent words. This is the big city after all; they've heard worse.

"Me, too," Ty says, and then he smiles, dimples and all. "But she's just the tip of the iceberg, Never. There is so much worse I could tell you." I look at Ty, and I want to put my hands over my ears, lock him out, forget this ever happened, but I can't because he needs to tell me. He needs to spill his secrets, so that I can carry half of them. I love him enough to know that he needs me and take a big breath. *Is this what a mother does for her child? Loves unconditionally and without judgment? My mom didn't make it look so easy, but if your heart is there, then it is. It really, truly is.*

"Tell me then," I say to Ty. "Take me somewhere and tell me everything."

26

Hannah introduces me to a man named Dick Prick, fakest fucking pseudonym ever. Sounds kind of funny at first, but then you meet the guy and learn that he deals in underage teens. Essentially, he's a fucking pimp. Hannah tells Dick Prick about me and buys me a nice dress shirt. She has me fuck her from behind in a dressing room at the place and then leaves, passing Dick two hundred bucks as she goes. I get twenty of it. Dick says he has the customers, and I've got the goods, and so he's going to take a percentage and if I'm good and check in with him when I'm supposed to, I'll get bonuses.

What Dick doesn't tell me is that during these check-ins, I have to suck his dick.

The first time it happens, I'm pretty shocked, but then Dick tells me that it's all a part of survival of the fittest or some shit. If that fucker wasn't already dead, baby, I'd kill him, too. He OD'd right after I left for California. Anyway, Nev, that was just the beginning of a three year stint where I ran tricks for Dick Prick and blew my money on pot, cigarettes, and alcohol. I didn't touch the harder stuff though I had plenty of opportunities to. Something told me that there was an invisible line between Hell and oblivion and as long as I stayed on the infernal side, I was fixable. I could end it someday. If I crossed over, I was going to end up dead in a gutter, a useless, broken, doll, a shell of a fucking person.

I did men mostly at first, but soon, I had transitioned over to female clients exclusively. The perverts had finally come out of the woodwork and showed me that the opposite sex can be just as cruel. I did whatever they told me to, no matter what it was, no matter how depraved or sick or fucked up. I did it until it changed from hurting myself to hurting others.

There was this couple, okay? And they had a third person with them, a woman. She was bound and gagged, spread open on a bed. I'd seen plenty of bondage before, so that was nothing new, but then ... I saw her face, her eyes. I'd seen her on the news a few weeks prior. She'd gone missing on her way home from the gym. I looked her right in the face, and I left. I ran, and I took all the money I had and booked a one way ticket to San Fran.

I left her there, Never. I left her there and I didn't tell anybody because I was afraid. Afraid of Dick Prick and the couple and even the cops when they found out that I was a runaway, a whore, an alcoholic. Two weeks later, they found her body. I'm responsible, baby. Me. I am. I could've saved her, and I didn't. I have her blood on my hands. Do you still love me? Do you still want me? How the fuck could you? And even if you do, you have to know that one day, I will go to Hell for all the things I have done. I will burn forever, and there is nobody that can save me.

27

Ty and I are sitting on the front porch of the house that is now ours according to his mother's lawyer. He tells me that he got a phone call while I was sleeping in the car, and that's how he knows. I don't give a shit about that right now. I don't care about the smell from the house or the fact that my phone is beeping nonstop, filled with texts from my sisters and Lacey, from Noah. I don't care about the little, orange tabby cat that's rubbing on my ankles or the small flakes of snow that are beginning to drift from the sky.

Ty stares blankly ahead of himself, eyes wide, hands shaking, and he lights up a cigarette. He smokes it quick and starts in on another. I don't blame him. How could I? The worst part about all of this is that he isn't even done. There's *more* to Ty's story. More pain, more heartache, more blood splattered across the walls of his heart. How did he ever live to tell the tale? That's what I need to know. I touch my SOG chip for reassurance, slide my fingers down my arm and pause when I reach my opposite hand, find the rings that Ty gave me and find strength in the undiscriminating metal.

"You were a kid, Ty," I tell him which he already knows. He turns to me like a zombie, neck stiff, muscles taught and I see that his lip ring is bloody from where he's chewed his lip to bits. I reach out and cover his mouth with my hand, trying stop him from hurting himself. Thus far, he's bounced back quick, but then, none of his revelations have been quite like this. I think of that poor girl, and I hope she didn't suffer long, that somehow, she knows that Ty didn't mean to abandon her there. They're both victims, Ty and that poor girl. I wish she were here, so she could forgive him, and maybe then he could move past this. For now, I'm afraid we've hit a dead end, that Ty is going to revert back. I pray that I'm wrong.

"Tyson Monroe McCabe," I say, but he isn't looking at me. His eyes are facing me, and they're open, yes, but he isn't seeing me. He's seeing that girl and he's wondering how much she suffered, and he's blaming himself for everything. But he's not a bad person, not my Ty McCabe. It's not just because I love him or because I feel sorry for him, not because he's my twisted, melted, bloodied, bandaged, fucked, mangled, burnt, screwed, slaughtered other half. It's because I can see it in his face. If he could go back in time, he would change everything, even if it damned him, even if he suffered for it, he would. "Regrets are the most important tools in the world, Ty

McCabe. If we didn't regret then mistakes would be nothing but a series of unstoppable accidents. We can regret something, and we can learn from it. Once we do though, once we understand why we regret something, we have to let it go. If you keep it, it will burn you. If you let it fly, it will become something else, something not quite as ugly or as perverted, but rather something new. That energy can rejoin the rest of the universe and be reborn. That's the whole point, isn't it? Change, rebirth, life." I grab Ty's hand and put it on my belly. "You can't check out on us now, McCabe. You started something new, and I'll be damned if I'm going to let you leave it unfinished."

My lover turns to me, eyes cloudy and he blinks, once, twice, three times, and then he's pulling me onto my lap and kissing me. He kisses me mouth and my cheeks and my forehead and my nose. He lays me flat on the wooden floor of the porch and pushes aside the fabric that separates us, drives into me, and fucks me right there in front of the neighborhood, hidden only by a bit of hedge. He takes me hard and fast, and I know that he isn't all there, that he's trying to dump his pain and sorrow, but that's okay. He took mine before, more than once, and now, I'm ready to take his. I said that recycling was a good thing, and I meant it. I will recycle Ty's memories into new things, better things, and he will do the same for me because that's what soul mates do.

When he's done, when he rolls off and slams into the wood, puts his hands to his face and screams, I let him. In fact, after a moment, I scream, too, and we come full circle. We come from being crazy college kids screaming in the middle of campus to lovers with a kid on the way, a house full of memories, and a dog who shares a name with my mother but who will forever "wear it best" so to speak because she loves unconditionally. We come full circle and I know that after the storm, there will be a rainbow.

28

Days pass before Ty is comfortable enough to continue on with his story. I don't push him. What I said before still stands. If he breaks himself into pieces for me, I will never forgive myself and he may never recover, so much as I need to hear the end of this, to finally lay it to rest and give it closure, I wait.

Noah gives us permission to stay as long as we need, ponying up money for the hotel, for the car, for the dumpster that Ty and I have to rent to clean up this damned house. I know he doesn't like to accept money from my ex, but he does it because that's the smart thing to do. We can save what little money he does have for the baby's things, for the nursery that lies hidden somewhere in the garbage up the stairs. Ty promises Noah that he'll pay him back when he strikes it rich. I don't know when that will be or how he'll do that, but I believe him. I believe him enough that I drag out bottles filled with yellow liquid. There's a whole mountain of them next to the bathroom that doesn't work, that has no running water, hasn't in years from the looks of it. Inside these plastic containers are piss. Urine. Pee. Wee. Whatever. Ty's mom really lost it there in the end. The sight of them sent him spiraling into a fit of rage wherein he took out a whole box of china to the yard and smashed it against the fence. I let him. I let him, and I took over, wearing nothing but a shirt tied around my face to block the smell. I only do it when he's not looking because he asked me not to. He's worried about the baby which I understand, but I'm more worried about his sanity, so I do it.

"I knew the bitch was nuts, but fuck me," Ty says as I surreptitiously hide the jug of piss I'm holding behind my back and crane my neck to see what he's uncovered in the downstairs bathroom. In the toilet bowl, which, of course, is long dry, there's a mountain of brand new toothbrushes. They're all still boxed up, wrapped in shiny plastic. Ty digs them out, cringing even though he's wearing some heavy duty gloves and throws them in the black trash bag to his left. "When I was a kid, she always bought toothbrushes when we went to the store. I mean, like lots of them. She used a new one every Goddamn day. But the amount I've found thus far defies logic. And to store them in the toilet bowl?"

"Hoarding," I say, thinking about what I've read on my phone in the few, quiet moments Ty and I spend together at the hotel. For the most part, we get up, we fuck, we eat, we clean, we eat again, we fuck, we sleep. Five days now we've done this same routine. "It sort of defies logic. It's a mental disorder."

"No shit," Ty says as he shoves a questionable bucket into his bag. It's stained with ... *matter* that I'd rather not discuss. "Psychotic bitch. Pedophile fucker. Useless whore." Ty rants like this pretty often when we're here, and to be honest, I get it. I mean, this place is fucking *sick*. I try to think up something to distract him.

"At least you had toothbrushes. My mom made us use miswaks." Ty is in a pissy mood, shoveling old clothing into his bag, but for this, at least, he pauses. "You'd think a Midwestern girl would be chill with Colgate or Crest or some shit, but not my mom." I sigh. *I really do hate that bitch.*

"'Kay," Ty says, standing up, brushing hair away from his sweaty head with the back of his hand. "What the fuck is a *miswak*?" I laugh and turn away so that I can get the piss jug into my garbage bag before Ty sees.

"It's a stick with fibers on the end. You chew it, and it's supposed to clean your teeth better than a toothbrush." Ty laughs which is a nice sound to hear. When we're in this house, he rarely laughs. I think the garbage sucks the joy right of him. I don't blame him for that, but if I find out that it's more than just the trash, if it's the house itself and the memories attached to it, I will drag his ass out of here faster than you can say *sex addict*.

"Sounds hot," Ty says as he strips off his gloves and glances over at the staircase. We've cleared it all the way up the top floor, but we haven't ventured any further. Ty is worried about the structural integrity of the building, or so he says. Honestly, I think that's a load of bullshit. I think that if I wasn't pregnant, he'd have dragged me up there right away, just to see the state of it. I mean, it's cute and all that he wants to protect me, but I've already told him twice that I am not going to break if he touches me the wrong way. I could probably get hit by a taxi cab and give birth to twins or some shit. "Did she make you stuff sea sponges up your cunt when you were on the rag, too?" I snort and wonder how the hell Ty gets these ideas in his head.

"You're a weirdo."

"I read an article about it once. It's supposed to be real good for your kitty cat."

"Fuck off." I follow Ty's lead and strip my gloves, toss them in the garbage bag and make my way outside onto the porch. The snow here is virginal, white and pretty as fuck. In the city, it's gray and slushy. I admire the contrast though I must admit that I prefer it here. It's quiet, it's serene, it's safe. I can see this house being perfect. I can imagine the fireplace roaring and Ty's hot body atop mine. I can even imagine holding a baby (though that's a bit of a stretch) on my lap while I enjoy the upstairs balcony that I haven't yet seen though Ty tells me has the best of views.

"How about fuck on?" he asks me as he wraps his arms around my waist. I'm not complaining, but Ty's been extra clingy lately, very touchy-feely, like he can't get enough of me. It's a distraction technique, a tactic to forget his pain which is fine, but that which I know I can't nurture for an extended period of time. Still, how mad can I be with tortured, tatted, pierced bad boy McCabe nibbling my earlobe?

"Maybe after you get me a cup of coffee," I say as I stretch my arms above my head. I get more and more tired everyday. Beth says it's because I'm 'cooking' the baby in my belly right now, forming a whole human being out of a cluster of cells. She says it's actually not so bad later on. I don't believe her. Beth doesn't even have stretch marks. Never trust a mother without stretch marks. Ty kisses my shoulder and moves off the porch and into the snow, promptly falls onto his back and makes a friggin' snow angel.

"Be spontaneous with me," he calls as I tuck my woolen coat tighter around me and descend into the powdery white fluff that is too picture perfect for words. I lay down next to Ty, and he starts to talk.

29

Let's end this now, Nev. I am so tired of carrying this around. I want to get rid of my pain and break out of my cocoon, spread my wings and fly free. I want to be like one of the fucking butterflies that are etched into my skin. I want to change, to know that I'm different inside and out, and then I want to grow old as fuck with you. I want to see your face tell a story with wrinkles and know that you're just as beautiful then as you are now, maybe even more so because I know that every day I spend with you, I get more and more attached.

Even now, the thought of being separated from you is unfucking-fathomable. If you die, I die. Literally. I will slit my own wrists, do it up Romeo and Juliet style. Call me unhealthy or obsessed or whatever, but it's true, and I won't apologize for it. What I will do is tell you the rest of this story and be done with it.

So, I failed that girl in the worst way possible and ran to San Francisco with twenty bucks in my pocket and a broken heart in my chest. I thought about starting over there, but it wasn't long before necessity and old habits took over my better judgment and sent me back to the streets. The going was tough though, tougher than back home. There weren't as many people willing to pay for it, so I slept on a park bench for a few weeks until I had enough money to travel. Then I took a bus and got off at the last stop, right outside a university in a city I'd never heard of.

I started working the streets on my own, relying on men while I was young and then, as I matured, I found that many of them were less interested in me, so I switched back to women. I changed from prostitute to escort and back again, more times than I can count. I lived in beach side manors with ladies who had too much money to spend by themselves, whose husbands had hordes of their own mistresses. I was an emotional tool as much as I was a physical one. On the opposite end of the spectrum, I'd take a couple hundred bucks cash and I'd fuck chicks against alley walls, in the backs of clubs, bathrooms. I know you don't want to hear this, Never, but I have to tell you. And if you think about it, this story really does have a happy ending because I found you. Let me keep going because I'm almost done, and then I'll never speak of it again. I won't want to, and I'll beg you not to. If there's anything you want to know, ask me now because then I'm done with this shit. I'm going to forget it completely, let my mind heal over the wounds and scab. I want to forget the sounds that people in pain make when they're trying to escape. I want to forget about the day that I stopped taking money for sex, went to work at the grocery store, and continued to fail myself. I sought out girls that mirrored my own pain, ones that I actually found attractive for once in my fucking life, and I was a fucking dick to them.

I had a lot of one night stands and quickie flings. I made people cry, broke hearts that were weak, and I felt good doing it. Misery loves company, right? I'm not proud of it, but it's true. Even you, Nev. I spotted you from across that room, and I knew that you were a bomb waiting to explode, a girl whose past was hotter than hell, a burning abyss of loss and anger and pain. I went up to you intending to do what I always did, and then I saw your eyes. Maybe you don't believe me because I didn't act like it, but I was affected by your face, your mouth, your skin, the sprinkle of freckles on your upper back. Never, when I asked you to go dancing with me, I had no idea what words were coming out of my mouth. When you responded back to me, I could tell that you didn't feel the same way, that you still wanted to use me to satisfy your own aching, emptiness. That's why I rejected you at first.

Then I saw you at that convenience store and everything changed. I wanted to save you, to get to know you. Something inside of me called for something you had inside of you. Everything that happened after that, I consider a blessing because it brought us together. You were the reason I wanted to change myself once and for all. After we fucked the first time, I knew I could never touch another woman and be happy. I needed you. I wanted you. I still do, Never, and that will never change.

30

"You believe me, don't you?" Ty asks as he rolls over and lays himself across my chest, presses his head to my breasts and breathes out a deep, deep sigh, one that I can tell he's been holding in for awhile. Tears are running down my face, hot and wet, and I have to dash them away before I address Ty, before I tell him that I love the fuck out of him, that there will never be another man for me, just him, always him. I think briefly about Noah Scott, but I know that if I had chosen him,

I would've been unhappy, always pining for that bit of molten heat that Ty possesses, that inner confidence that gives his full lips sexy grins and his makes my body go up in flames at the simplest of touches.

"Of course," I tell him because I know he would never lie to me. We are way past that shit. Everything is out in the open now, and it feels so damn good. I would liken it to an orgasm of the spirit, this viciously peaceful awakening that makes the senses tingle and the world explode in light and color that washes away the darkness and lights up the earth with brilliance. "How could I doubt you after that?"

"I could be full of shit," he mumbles, sounding sleepy, like he can't bear to keep his eyes open any longer. "I could be lying to you, telling you what you want to hear."

"No," I say firmly. "That's not true."

"How do you know?" he asks me, challenging my affection, my trust, as is his right. I have tested him over and over and over and each time, he's passed with flying colors. What makes this any different? At least he's not pulling out an old flame on me, making me go on hikes with her, inviting her and her dog over to his family's house to hang out. I am beyond cruel. Poor Ty.

"Because," I say to him as I push him off into the snow. "You never tell me what I want to hear." Ty laughs and just lays there in his black coat and red scarf with his stupid holey jeans and signature combat boots. He looks like an ad for a winter catalog, a sexy one, one where the cover is the only page where the men are wearing clothes. I am one lucky girl. "You cuss too much, use my razor to shave your chest." Ty starts to protest, but I hold up a hand to shush him. "You're inappropriate and dangerous as hell. You're exactly the kind of guy that mothers warn their daughters about." I pause. "On the outside that is. On the inside, you have a soul that's desperate to love and be loved, to appreciated and be appreciated. You want to belong somewhere and you want to be something. We can all relate to that. You're not so different after all, Mr. McCabe." He lays there silently for a moment and then sits up, scooting through the snow until our thighs touch. It's cold as hell out here but neither of us notice as snowflakes catch on eyelashes, ears, hair, as they float around like confetti and decorate our clothes with white polka dots. We're too busy staring at one another, readjusting, figuring out what it's like to be happy. When you live your whole live being miserable, it's a bit uncomfortable to switch gears, to stretch yourself open and feel something you've never felt before. Love sets broken bones, and yes, eventually, we will feel good again, whole, but for now, it hurts and that's okay. That is o-fucking-kay.

"Is there anything you want to know?" Ty whispers, dark eyes sliding away from me and over to the dumpster that holds the trash from the kitchen, the living room, and the bathroom. We have a long way to go in cleaning this place, but in a way, I like that. I'm putting elbow grease and time into a treasure that means something to Ty, that has the potential to make him happy, to make me happy. I think about Ty's question for a long while, certain that he's serious about closing the door on this case. If there I anything that I'm wondering about, that I need to understand, I better ask it now. If I don't, and I try to bring it up again, I will wound Ty in ways that even I will be hard pressed to understand. So I think and I think and I think. I think about asking him how many people he slept with, if it felt good, how much money he made, what that girl's name was ... that, poor, poor girl. I think about asking him if he was ever raped on the streets, how he managed to stay sane, how he came to the decision to work at the grocery store. There's a lot there that's missing. It's like Ty's given me the outline of his life, and he hasn't written the book yet. I know though that as curious as I might be in the future, as much as I might want to ask for that manuscript, that I won't. There are some things that are not meant to be read, some secrets that are meant to remain buried, forgotten, lost. I let the door slam on Ty's past, and I like that some of it is still a mystery to me. It makes him sexier somehow, more interesting.

I smile.

"I have one question," I ask him and he cringes. I move forward, straddle Ty's lap and wiggle until I feel his body respond to me, pressing hard and insistent against the heat between my thighs.

"Yeah?" he asks, voice tentative, afraid.

"What's your preference: girl or boy?"

31

Ty doesn't care if our kid is a boy or a girl and neither do I. Gender is irrelevant in the world of love. Love exists pure and perfect without expectations or rules or restrictions. People put them there sometimes, try to map out the path of an energy that is too pure and perfect to restrain. That's how they get themselves into trouble. Neither McCabe nor I will make that mistake. And we certainly won't repeat the mistakes of those around us. We won't emulate my mother's selfish, illusive tendencies or his mother's blind, single-mindedness.

This is the kind of stuff we talk about while we clean that house. We don't talk about ultrasounds or doctors or midwives or any of that shit. We discuss philosophy and poetry and politics and get deeper and deeper into one another. Elbow deep in muck and discarded kitsch, Ty and I grow closer and closer, open up wide like flowers in the sun and drink in one another's energy. Oh yeah. And we fuck, too. We fuck on the elevator at the hotel, in the stairwell, in the car, in the snow. By the time the week is up, I'm so sore I can barely walk and Ty's baby is cranky as hell, forcing me to drink fruit smoothies by the gallon and sit on a folding chair while he shovels old newspaper and empty tin cans. If I bend over, I puke. Period.

The downstairs is now mostly clean, and I have even penned my first poem. It isn't very good, but Ty likes it. He sing-songs the lines as he scrubs down walls, floors, counters. He doesn't complain as he does it either, seemingly rather joyous in his discovery that, unlike the horrible *Hoarders* show we've been watching at night in the hotel (postcoital, mind you), this house has survived. Ancient craftsmanship combined with a shorter duration of the horde and the fact that the upstairs is not full of garbage, merely stuff, makes taking over this place as our future home a real possibility.

I spend my days laughing and my nights listening to Ty's charcoal voice slither through the empty places in my being, warming them up, melting me, and reshaping me into the woman I want to become. I think we're going to get a happy ending, Ty and me. He's going to become a therapist for troubled teens and me, I'm going to do something reckless and artistic, something that makes no money, but it won't matter because I'll have my tortured bad boy and a baby and a dog. Oh yeah, and that orange tabby cat. It sits on the bottom step and watches us day in and day out. I told Ty not to feed it, so it would go home, but he didn't listen. Later, much later, we found a picture of it in a drawer, so we think it belonged to Ty's mom. He says he's naming it Chuck Norris, but we'll see about that.

We'll see about a lot of things, Ty and me, but that's okay, we have time. We have forever.

Epilogue

Never is too tapped out for this shit, so I'm going to take over. She just had a fucking, baby, okay? My baby. He's wrapped up now in blankets with butterflies, and he's the most beautiful creature I've ever seen – except for her. Except for Never Ross-McCabe, my wife. That's right, I had a JOP come down here stat, and he married us literally hours before our son came into the world. His name is Noah which was my choice, not hers. I can appreciate a man with a passion and as happy as I am to have won, I can't help but realize how much he might have been hurt by losing her. So Never and I have a kid named after her ex. It's kind of fucked, but hey, so are we. We've come a long way, true, but we've got a long way to go which is good because if there was nowhere else to go, life would get pretty boring pretty quick.

The Regali clan is going to come up and visit, throw us a housewarming party, so I hear. At least, that's what we're telling Never. I've got a lot of other cool shit planned. Remember that dress, that white one that she didn't want to wear? Well, I bought it and I'll be damned if I don't see her in our backyard under an archway of black, fucking roses.

You want me to give you a happy ever after or some shit? Am I right? Well, I can't do that. I can give you a happy for now because that's all there really is to life. We have to live in the moment and make the best decisions that we know how. What I can do is promise you that I will love that woman forever, that I'd rather die than do something stupid that could hurt her. I can tell you that she changed my life, and I think, somehow, I changed hers. We're good for each other, Never and me. Just two tortured souls tangled together for life. Just two, tortured fucking souls in love.

THE END

or

is it?

Want to know what happens to Noah and Zella? How about India? Did you guys get enough Ty and Never? Send an email to author@cmstunich.com with your requests and we'll see where the wind takes us. After all, it's about living in the moment. You talk; I'll listen. And readers, one last note:

I heart the fuck out of you.

If you enjoyed this book, look for

Paint Me Beautiful:
A Tale of Anorexia, a Love Story, and the Rebirth of Claire Simone

*Coming March 2013!
Excerpt included*

CHAPTER ONE

All journeys have to start somewhere.

In my experience, they usually begin where you least expect them, peeping out from behind corners and under rugs. They grab you by the ankle and take you to places you'd never thought you'd go, and they don't care if you're already heading somewhere, if you've already mapped out your future. When fate takes control, you can either ride with it or fight against it. I chose to fight, but we'll talk about that later. For now, let's talk about Emmett Sinclair.

He's tall, almost as tall as me when I'm wearing my best heels. He has these eyes that can pierce your soul if you let them, like he's just in tune with the universe and everything in it. Maybe that's how he spotted me, chose me, made me the center of his world? I guess I'll never know because the day he first notices me, I barely even see him.

I'm standing in line with a group of pretty girls. They've all got perfect hair and perfect teeth and smooth skin, like cream or cocoa or bronze. I'm comparing myself to every single one of them, starting with the blonde in front and working my way back. *I am so out of my league,* I think as I examine the redhead two ahead of me in line. She's at least ten pounds thinner than I am and she has this lanky-pretty quality that I've seen in a lot of magazines lately, like she was born skinny, not made skinny.

I adjust the straps of my tank top and I hope I look

appropriate. My blonde hair is slicked back into a ponytail and I've got on a pair of size two jeans. I wish they were smaller. In fact, I'm utterly convinced that I'm going to be passed over because I'm too fat. I made the journey out here anyway. It was either that or sit at home and make peanut butter cookies with my mom, defend myself for not wanting to taste something made with two sticks of butter. I shift back and forth as a murmur passes down the line of girls.

"No thank you," they're all saying. I turn around and find a boy. It's Emmett Sinclair, but I don't know that yet, not until he gets to me with a red tray in his hand a black beanie on his head. Tufts of chestnut hair stick out in random places, just enough that it gives him this messy-cute look. Any longer and he'd look scruffy, but he's clean shaven and his shirt is crisp and clean. He's also wearing a red apron with a *Super Smoothie* logo on it.

"Good afternoon," he says, and the words come out of my mouth automatically.

"No thank you." I can't drink one of those cups, not when I'm seconds away from finding out if my destiny is in reach, if I'll be one of those girls that you hear about, the ones that get discovered in a mall. They start in modeling and work their way up to TV, film, music. A triple threat they used to call them – dance, act, sing – but the stakes are even higher now. To be that girl, the one that they all look at, that they all want to be, you have to be beautiful, more beautiful than they are because it's the only way you'll stand out.

"Are you sure?" he asks, and in his voice, I can see that he's trying to flirt with me.

He's cute, so I say, "Catch me after this? My stomach's in knots, and I can't think straight." I don't have time for cute, but there it is.

"Emmett Sinclair," he says, and he doesn't move away. I smile nice and tight, but I can't stop looking at the girls that are walking down the faux runway they've set up in the middle of the food court with butcher paper. It's been taped to the linoleum floor nice and tight, but it's not enough to keep the stilettos from tearing it here and there as the girls stomp their way down to the end, pose, and turn. "Your turn," the boy continues and although I'm barely listening to him, I respond.

"Claire," I say. "Claire Simone." Emmett chuckles and tugs down the front of his beanie. He's totally feeling me now, but I barely see him. I see long legs and skinny bodies and desperation that mirrors my own. God, they want this so bad. Almost as much as I want it. Almost. Nobody wants this like I do. I want to be seen; I want to be beautiful. I want to be that girl that other girls look at and wish they were. Why? I don't know. I'm not a ward of the state or a victim of abuse or anything like that. I'm a girl with two loving parents and a big sister who's sweet, if a bit pushy. Something inside of me just wants to be seen, and there's nothing wrong with that, is there?

"Sinclair and Simone," Emmett says, and I turn my face slightly to look at him. My stomach is twisting and clenching, giving me the world's worst cramps. I fight them back and try to ignore Emmett as he balances his tray from one hand to the other. "Sounds tragic, don't you think?"

"Mm hmm," I say, but I'm no trying to be rude. I'm not trying to be anything. I just want to get through this with a nod or a smile from the panel of men and women that sit behind that long table and stare. I want one, just one, of them to come up to me and say, *Wow, Claire, you are it. You are the next big thing.* I don't think I can handle anymore rejection.

This is my fifth casting this week, and if I don't sign with an agency soon, my mother is going to really set in on me about choosing a different career path.

The line scoots forward and Emmett follows. His samples are melting, but I don't think he cares. *This guy is really into me,* I think, but I can't be happy about that because it's almost my turn to walk. My runway walk is not my best attribute. I take great pictures though. At least, I've been told that before. I'm both commercial and high fashion say the agencies who never sign me. I sigh and shift my portfolio from one arm to the other.

"Is this for *America's Next Top Model*?" he asks, and I don't sigh or roll my eyes like the girl in front of me does. I smile softly and shake my head.

"Not quite, no," I say, and Emmett nods. His brown eyes are curious though, but he can tell I'm way too deep into this right now to flirt with him, so he takes a step back.

"Good luck, Claire," he tells me and moves over to a table to sit down. I wonder what his boss at the *Super Smoothie* thinks about that, but I can't really focus on him right now. I need to keep myself focused. *Think tall, think pretty, think perfect.* I swallow hard and close my eyes for a second to get control over myself.

"Next."

That one word, so simple, draws me forward with the skinny redhead and the girl between us, the one that I think is pretty, but is too short. Agencies don't like short. They don't like fat either, so I make a point to suck in my stomach as I approach the butcher paper and step onto it, unconsciously memorizing the rips and tears, so I don't have to look down while I'm walking. That's the sign of a real, true supermodel.

I lay my portfolio down slowly, purposely letting

the other girls set theirs down first. These people have been staring at pretty pictures all day, and they don't have the time nor the patience to sit and examine each one. If they're only going to glance at one of our portfolios, I want it to be mine. I feel bad for the other two girls, but I've had worse done to me, so I decide this is just karma. The redhead looks familiar to me anyhow, and I wouldn't be surprised if she'd sabotaged me before.

"Set up at the end of the runway, please. Hold your pose and turn back. When you're finished, please come back up and grab your portfolios. We'll call you." The woman who's speaking sounds bored and looks it, too. Her eyes take us all in, judge us in a split second. She doesn't need to see us walk; she already knows, and I can tell she doesn't like me. *It's because I'm so fat. That's why.* I feel so guilty over the food I ate last night that I makes me sick. I had cheese. I shouldn't have had cheese.

I march to the end of the runway and spin, letting my hair flow out behind me. I have nice hair; I've always had nice hair. Unfortunately, with extensions and weaves and all that, it doesn't really matter. Hair is fixable. Fat is not – not on a runway. I try to tell myself that I look good, that I look professional. I've got on new skinny jeans, new shoes, just a bit of light foundation. I look polished.

It's not enough.

The woman at the end of the panel motions for us to move forward, and we do, in perfect unison I might add. At first, the short girl keeps up with us, but soon, our long legs move the redhead and I past her. I make sure to swing my arms a bit, but not too much. I don't want to look like an ape. My strides are long and graceful and my eyes are focused on a man with a goatee who I think might be straight. You never know in this industry, but it's worth a try. I could never do anything like sleep my way to the top, but if it's just a bit of eye contact, that's okay.

I pause, put one hand on my hip and tilt my chest side to side, popping my shoulder forward and my ass back, just enough so that I look shapely, but not too shapely. I've been practicing this walk for ages, and I hope to hell it's paid off. It may not be my best skill, but if it's good enough and my pictures are good enough, maybe they'll take me on.

I turn and out of the corner of my eye, I see Emmett clapping. He's the only one doing it, and it's a little weird, but it makes me smile. Good thing the agency reps can't see my face now. I hit the end of the runway and pose again. I'm staring at a faux wall that's been constructed to give a slight bit of privacy to us in this busy commercial hub. There are people leaning over the railings from above and gaping from either side of the runway, but that's okay. That's what we're here for: to be looked at.

I turn around again, still a model, still perfection in heels, and walk right back towards that panel like I'm stomping for Alexander McQueen or something. The other girls are not following suite, so I know that I am standing out, for better or worse. When I hit the table, I don't pose, just reach out and grab my portfolio. It hasn't been touched. That much is obvious.

"Thank you," I mumble along with the other girls. Nobody stops me as I walk away. Right off the bat, I begin to analyze my performance. Did I walk too fast? Too slow? Did I swing my arms enough?

"You were really great," Emmett says as I pause next to him. Honestly, I had forgotten his existence. I feel a gentle flush warm my cheeks and try to give him a genuine smile.

"Thanks," I say as I reach up and let my hair

tumble down around my shoulders. I fluff it with my fingers and shake my head a bit. Emmett's brown eyes follow my motions, drink me in like I am the cat's meow. I like that, so my smile gets bigger all on its own. My sister thinks I'm narcissistic, but that isn't it at all. I'm just focused on my dreams and those dreams depend on my appearance, so I pay attention to it. That's all it is. My stomach growls a bit, and I lay my arm across it to keep it quiet.

"Want to grab something to eat?" Emmett asks, and I want to say yes, but I can't. I ate a lot this morning anyway, and my stomach is just riled up from all of the anxiety.

"Aren't you working?" I ask as I point a finger at his apron. Emmett pinches the straps with his fingers and grins at me. He has long canines that peek out of his lips a bit when he smiles. *Cute.*

"You mean this?" he asks as he drops the fabric and adjusts his beanie. "I'm just about to get off for lunch. Have you ever been to The Winged Ones? It's this fantastic sandwich shop that has a roof garden upstairs. It's a diamond in the rough, really. My treat." His offer is appealing, to be sure, but I have an early morning casting, and I can't be tired or I get these massive bags under my eyes. It's an open call for a print campaign, too, which is rare and not something I can screw up. I bite my lip gently and try to let him down easily. He really is nice.

"I can't," I say and he groans, reaching up to pull his beanie over his face.

"It's the apron, isn't it?" he asks as I take a moment to admire the swell of his muscular arms and the way his right eye peeks out from beneath the black knitted hat to examine me. "Hey, I understand though. You're wondering why you should be interested in a guy who works at the *Super Smoothie*, right?" I chuckle and shake my head.

"Not at all," I say because that isn't it. I just have other things on my mind right now. First and foremost is how I'm going to be able to skip out of family dinner again. I've gotten away with it six days in a row, but tonight, Marlena is coming over, and there is no way she's going to miss my absence. Unfortunately, Mom has also chosen tonight to make her famous fried chicken. All of that grease makes me sick to my stomach, but I know I won't be able to escape that table without eating at least a piece. Already, I feel nauseous. "I just have this family thing tonight, so ... " I trail off and tuck some hair behind my ear. I feel like I'm in high school again. "How about Friday?" I blurt before Emmett gets the chance to say anything else. He pulls his beanie off his head and lays it in his lap. His brown hair is mussy and totally sexy.

"Friday is perfect," he tells me and then passes me his phone. I plug in my number and hand it back to him. I could take his number, too, but I won't remember to call. It's nothing personal, but it's all up to him now. The ball is in his court. If he calls, I'll go. If he doesn't, then there will be others. Nothing against Emmett because he seems really nice and he's absolutely gorgeous, but I just don't have time to be serious with men right now. They are not my top priority; modeling is. *Fashion* is. "Hey, can I take your picture, too?" he asks as he shakes his phone back and forth with one hand.

"Why?" I ask as my eyes slide over to the line of girls that snake through the crumb covered tables in the food court, wind around the fountain near the escalators and trail back towards and inspiring window display of a local boutique. I hear they have some good stuff in there, and I've been meaning to go in for quite some time, but I'm just not happy with my body right now, and it's not fun to shop for clothes if you're not happy.

"You're so beautiful," Emmett says, but the words roll off me like water on a duck's feathers, just slide right over and down my sides, giving me the chills but little else. I don't feel beautiful. If I was, the agency reps would've smiled at me or at the very least looked at my portfolio. I glance over my shoulder briefly and see that the bored woman with the lumpy chin is no longer bored. She's standing up and grinning from ear to ear, shaking the hand of a waspish girl with big ears and squinty eyes. She's skinny though, much skinner than me, definitely a size zero. People can talk all they want about the industry changing and about bans on too thin models, but that's just in the big games, just for show. Back here, at the starting line, it's all about skinny. It has been ever since Twiggy emerged as the new pretty, when Marilyn Monroe was out, and rail thin became in. "You know what?" Emmett says as he stands up and grabs his red tray in one hand. "Don't respond to that." He spins the tray around with his other hand which is actually quite impressive and makes me smile. "That was weird. I don't know why I even said that." Emmett chuckles and winks at me as he turns away. "See you on Friday," he calls over his shoulder as he slides his beanie over his head with his other hand.

"See you on Friday," I say.

About the Author

C.M. Stunich was raised under a cover of fog in the area known simply as Eureka, CA. A mysterious place, this strange, arboreal land nursed Caitlin's (yes, that's her name!) desire to write strange fiction novels about wicked monsters, magical trains, and Nemean Lions (Google it!). She currently enjoys drag queens, having too many cats, and tribal bellydance.

She can be reached at author@cmstunich.com, and loves to hear from her readers. Ms. Stunich also wrote this biography and has no idea why she decided to refer to herself in the third person.

Happy reading and carpe diem!

www.cmstunich.com

Made in the USA
Lexington, KY
11 March 2013